THE PREDATOR

Books by Linda Grace Hoyer

ENCHANTMENT

THE PREDATOR

The

PREDATOR

Linda Grace Hoyer

with drawings by
Elizabeth Updike Cobblah

TICKNOR & FIELDS
New York • 1990

For information about permission to reproduce selections
from this book, write to Permissions, Ticknor & Fields,
215 Park Avenue South, New York, New York 10003.

Library of Congress Cataloging-in-Publication Data

Hoyer, Linda Grace.
  The predator / Linda Grace Hoyer.
    p.   cm.
  ISBN 0-89919-923-2
  I. Title.
PS3558.0947P74   1990   89-37704
813'.54 — dc20   CIP

Printed in the United States of America
Book design by Robert Overholtzer

P 10 9 8 7 6 5 4 3 2 1

Six of these chapters appeared in
somewhat different form in *The New Yorker.*

For John and Martha

Contents

If you are lonely enough, you will never know lonesomeness,
With day full of leaves that whisper, and night never visionless.

— Robert Penn Warren

You can live a lifetime and, at the end of it, know more about
other people than you know about yourself. You learn to watch
other people, but you never watch yourself because you strive
against loneliness. If you read a book, or shuffle a deck of cards,
or care for a dog, you are avoiding yourself. The abhorrence of
loneliness is as natural as wanting to live at all.

— Beryl Markham

THE PREDATOR

The Predator

YESTERDAY, while mousing in the meadow, Ezra saw a car drift down the road and, remembering that cars now carry men with guns, he ran toward the barn. Looking into the meadow from an upstairs room of the house, Ada saw his body extended in the graceful forward motion that for almost twelve years had set him apart from the clumsy men who came to the farm with dogs and guns to kill. One of these men, having come to Ada's back door to explain his intention to kill the mourning doves that he had seen feeding in a nearby cornfield, said, "A dove is one of the fastest targets we have. So you needn't be afraid that I'll shoot all of them. The average hunter is happy if he gets a dozen of the weak and the old — birds that will be killed by predators anyway." And Ada had believed him, knowing that for each of us there is a predator and the game of life is nothing more than an attempt to postpone the day when predator and prey meet.

Yet she had said, "Please don't shoot the doves in that cornfield. Let them live as long as they can." Laughing, this hunter had left the house and taken his party to other, presumably greener, cornfields.

That was the fall Ezra was born. And now it was spring, more than eleven years later, that time of the year when only red squirrels, raccoons, woodchucks, grackles, opossums, skunks — and cats — must be wary of men with guns. Knowing this, Ada was wary, too. Certainly the caution with which the driver of the car slowed to a stop where Ezra, with bristling fur, had taken flight was thought-provoking, even though Ada, unable to see the man's face, could not know what was in his mind. Since the car was a familiar sight in the neighborhood, it was possible that its driver, seeing Ezra, had stopped to say a kind word and praise him for his fine appearance. In fact, the words "he is admiring Ezra" had occurred to Ada and prevented her from leaving the house in a natural response to Ezra's flight.

Hearing the rifle, Ada ran, like Ezra, toward the barn, and there, in the barn's shadow, she saw Ezra — dying.

"Oh, Ezra. Ezra." For the rest of her life, Ada will hope that he heard her.

In the summer, when she will mow the grass that grows on his grave under the holly tree, Ada can be glad that the man who killed Ezra could shoot well enough to have spared him the pain of mutilation and slow death. Then, dry-eyed, she will think that Ezra died well and, aside from his premature weaning and later castration, lived well.

Sometimes, after a nap or a meal, he came to the sofa where Ada was catnapping and began "to nurse." At other times, he climbed into the laps of female guests in hopes of being held while he nursed. "Ezra thinks you are his mother," Ada said, removing him to the floor.

Recalling the laughter that had followed her remark, Ada now wonders why they laughed at Ezra, who, having survived the torments of his weaning and gelding, was able to go on living with grace and good humor. Why was she angry when he brought a young quail to the kitchen door for her? It was his quail that he had given to her. And why did her son, Christopher, sob, so that she thought their telephone connection was broken, when she told him that Ezra had died? Was it because he had given Ezra to her when he left home to go on that long trip from which they knew he would not return? There would be hurried visits and many letters, but no homecoming. Ezra had enjoyed the freedom Christopher's going gave him and, although a city cat, invaded the land and brought back from it gifts of cardinals, indigo buntings, and warblers until, on the first morning of his stay on the farm, the lawn was abloom with dead birds.

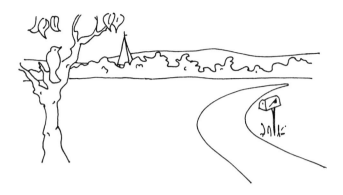

Primal Therapy

WHEN MARTY'S CARDIOLOGIST called to say that Marty was "breathing on his own now," or, as Ada herself would have said, "being allowed to die after his long illness and nine hours in intensive care," she thanked him and went to wait in her mother-in-law's wing chair. It was the chair in which her husband, if he had not preferred the hospital, might have waited for death. It was the chair in which a favorite aunt and his mother had waited and in which Marty, during the nights when his sense of being "full" was too oppressive to be borne in bed, had found relief.

Sitting there, Ada spoke his name and heard the sound of it in the quiet room with the kind of incredulous wonder that "goodbye" — shouted to a long-loved person at a considerable distance — often stirs.

5

But of course it was not the same as saying goodbye.

Marty had not gone away. The odor of his agony still surrounded her, and the chill of his hands was no less real than it had been when she touched them and left him. Dying.

"No, don't come," Marty's doctor had said. "I wouldn't want you to see him the way he is now."

So Ada waited in the big chair while an April thundershower washed the house and Marty died. When the telephone rang again, it was the doctor asking permission to perform an autopsy.

"Do you expect to learn something from it?" she asked, because it seemed unlikely that, after more than ten years in the doctor's care, Marty had anything further to teach him.

"We usually do."

"Then you may perform an autopsy."

Dry-eyed and speechless — except for her recurring tendency to repeat Marty's name — Ada went to bed. It was, she was certain, what Marty would have wanted her to do.

Three days later, feeling that Marty was pleased with the freedom he presumably now enjoyed, Ada listened to the funeral sermon that Pastor Neal was beginning to deliver:

"We are sad today because a teacher, churchman, civic leader, husband, father, grandfather, gentleman, and friend is no longer with us. His absence now will affect the family who loved him and lived with him and shared the unique qualities of his life. That absence will also affect the hundreds, even thousands of others who over the years came to know him and respect him and admire him for his never-ending kindness, for his uncommon modesty, and for his remarkable capacity to see some good in everybody he met. That this giant of a man — and I mean that literally and figuratively — is no longer a presence among us is just cause for us to be sad."

Ada could not help smiling inwardly at this. Whether she was relieved to see that Pastor Neal, whose eyes were brimming with tears, still was able to cry, or glad to remember that it was Marty's six feet two inches of height and the pride with which he carried it that had made him her husband, she could not have said. Certainly, along with the pastor's tears and her memory of the young man whose presence, indeed, had seemed gigantic, the sermon was a revelation so surprising that she wanted to laugh in the way small children laugh at a fairy tale.

Yet the pastor's eyes were full of tears and his voice was eloquent, speaking of a man she seemed to have known somewhat as she knew their mailman (a dependable man who came and went at predictable times with news both good and bad, sometimes angry but always aloof, a man whose real business had nothing to do with her) and less well, as a matter of fact, than she knew the heavyset plumber who came to deal with the unexpected failures of their electric pump.

On all sides of Ada, people were holding their handkerchiefs, ready to stanch the flow of tears and nasal excretions, when Pastor Neal said:

"But we are also glad today. For we can come into this church and make these statements because they are true. This is the church where he regularly worshipped for many years. This is the church where he faithfully taught the adult Bible class for a longer time than I can remember. This is the church where his extraordinary faith both in God and his fellow man was renewed and strengthened — through Word and Sacrament. We are glad today because we can rejoice in the memory of his Christian life and we can thank God that He made it possible for us to know this man and be enriched by him in so many ways."

Ada bowed her head and closed her eyes. The tremor of a petit mal came and went while she wondered if Marty's enrichment of the lives of these tearful people could have been a little like her own enrichment by the painting of Christ's transfiguration that, throughout her childhood, had been on the wall behind the altar. After a renovation of the church, the painting had been covered by an arras.

"We don't know anyone who restores that kind of painting," Ada had been told when she asked why the arras was needed.

"I'm so sorry," she had said, thinking of all the long sermons through which the representation of Jesus in a floating white garment, with the favored disciples — Peter, James, and John — in cloaks of Easter-egg coloring on a grassy slope below the unspeakable glory, had sustained her. "But the painting will always be there?"

"Yes. Under the arras," the woman who had bought the arras said.

Seated now in one of the pews where both Ada and the painting had once been considered stylish, she felt those early years — when her love had transfigured the world so that she could not fall asleep for fear that somehow, while she slept, the world and everyone in it might be lost — becoming more real than they recently had been. In those years, the painting, she supposed, had enriched her own life in a way roughly comparable to the way in which Marty had enriched Pastor Neal's life. It was natural, therefore, that he, an honest man determined to keep the scales in balance, should have seen the funeral sermon as an opportunity, perhaps an obligation, to transfigure Marty's life. If not an outright exaggeration of Marty's virtues, his speech was an irradiation of them. Or was it true — as one or two of Marty's old college friends had suggested, both before her marriage to Marty and afterward — that she was not really able to appreciate Marty?

No better equipped to answer that question than she had ever been, but still fascinated by the mass of its unknown quantities, Ada briefly considered the difference between Pastor Neal's appreciation of Marty's life in retrospect and her own. At his best, she had found Marty warmly exciting; at his worst, painfully irritating.

Yet in and under the roles of "street angel" and "house devil" — both of which Marty had played to perfection — there was a solidly masculine presence. It was this presence, she imagined, that Pastor Neal had discovered and was now describing. It was to this presence that Ada herself had addressed her proposals of marriage when one of Marty's long absences had convinced her that she could not live without him.

Almost all of those letters had been lost in Marty's progress from one place of employment to another, while almost all of his letters existed still, in one of the old trunks in the attic. During Marty's last illness, she untied one of the packages and found in it a letter of her own, written after a visit during which, quite obviously, their relationship had been weighed in the balance and found wanting. The letter's paper was the

green of a luna moth's wing and stiff with the courage
of youth. It began:

> Dearest Marty — In the most literal sense, you are
> all the world to me and the only desire or ambition I
> have is to help you to be happy. If you don't want to
> marry me, I'll find some other way to help you. This
> is what I've been wanting to tell you all summer.

Later — and even more incredibly — the letter
went on:

> I, too, wish that fate had made me your sister. But
> I'm not your sister. I'm Ada and have to make the
> best of it. I believed you when you said that it hurts
> you to be so far away. Yet whenever you mention
> marriage, you look terribly depressed. Why, Marty?

After thanking him for his visit, the letter ended
with a piece of advice that Marty, she was sure, could
not have taken seriously then, and that she, after more
than forty years as his wife, did not understand at all.

> Don't worry, darling, about your work — or
> anything. The only real wealth is time. Let's invest
> it where it gives us the most interest.
>
> Your own Ada.

A year later, with dozens of lesser letters in the
meantime, Marty had replied to that letter, having accepted the fact that Ada was not his sister and must,

therefore, become his wife. It was a twelve-page letter — the longest of their lengthy correspondence — and so plainly punctuated with the anguish of self-sacrifice that, while rereading it, Ada was as close to tears as sympathy for another human being could bring her.

After paying tribute to the memory of William Jennings Bryan (who had died the week before) and Ada's father (who was alive), Marty listed her virtues. Since the list was a short one, he had asked her to forgive his faults without listing them.

> I realize so many of them must be corrected, Ada. But now I understand how much it means to possess a superior mentality and I realize more and more — as I know you — how profitable and advantageous the application of knowledge is.

The problem of marrying her he had tackled manfully by writing a modified quotation of her father's endorsement of honesty as the best policy.

> As your daddy says, courage, stick-to-itiveness, and honesty win out in the end. What a true possessor of common sense that man is. I don't blame you for appreciating him.
>
> Dear, to write more would be only a repetition of the fact that I love you.
>
> I don't mean to be pessimistic. But living alone has been so distasteful to me.

Perhaps exhausted by the effort of writing at such length and supposing that somehow his faith in her father's judgment would suffice, Marty had ended with "Ada, yours till Judgment Day and through eternity."

Almost before the wedding ceremony could be performed, however, Ada had begun to wonder if Marty's promise to live with her forever was meant. As her husband, he had a penchant for saying things that, almost certainly, implied that her hopes of being helpful to him had not been realized. And when she asked him to explain, his answer was "My mother told me not to marry you. Because you are an idealist and I am not."

Happily, she had become somewhat used to her mother-in-law's view of their marriage before Marty was moved to say "Ada, there is no such thing as love. What 'love' means is nothing but a willingness to be exploited. And you're not willing to be exploited. In fact, you're the most completely selfish person I ever met."

This revelation of Marty's own view of the truth was related, she had thought, to the familiar belief that in some persons both a "street angel" and a "house devil" have made their home. Surely there were times when, loving the street angel in Marty, she had hated the house devil who lived with her.

So that, without the solidly masculine presence, dependable and strong, their marriage would have ended before it began. This was the presence that Pastor Neal had known and, with wet eyes, described. This was the man who, during their last meeting, had said, "Ada, I want to get well so that I can help you." This was the Marty who — coming and going like the mailman — would be with her "till Judgment Day." He would not want her to cry now.

Unlike Girls

WHEN CHRISTOPHER was six, Ada had often wondered what he was thinking as, safely across the busy street where they lived, his body became — suddenly and inexplicably — airborne before, like a cat returned to the ground from a tree, he ran toward the schoolhouse, where he was in the first grade. When Ada was six, she had loped to school without first bounding into the air. Not only were jumping and whistling believed to be "unbecoming to girls" when Ada was Christopher's age, the thought (whatever it was) that lifted her son would never have occurred to her so early in the morning of a school day. Even when the school day was over and she saw her father's house in the distance, her spirit invariably had kept one, or both, of her feet on the ground.

Her frequent glimpses of Christopher in levitation had, at first, surprised Ada, much as the sight of him in a red beard, thirty years later, did. Her acceptance of both surprises had been wordless. What, after all, could she have said?

"Boys will be boys," the old folks said when she was a child. And Ada, hearing them, had not, for one moment, doubted it. What girls would be was, it seemed, a matter of either conjecture or unspeakable concern to their parents. Otherwise, the old folks would have said, "Girls will be girls." But, having told her that boys will be boys, they said nothing more until some years later, when one of them told her, "Men want to do what they want to do when they want to do it. And you can't stop them." At this, Ada had smiled. It was too absurd to be believed. Everybody wanted to do what he or she wanted to do when he or she wanted to do it and no one really did. Men worked while women waited, and both accepted the results. Life was as simple as that.

This is not to say that Ada, having seen Christopher in levitation and bearded, was not to be surprised in other ways. Nothing could have been further from the truth. Scarcely a day had dawned and died without its surprise. It was impossible, now that she was *una anziana,* for her to remember them all. Of one surprise, however, she had a clear recollection and a memento, which stood on the kitchen shelf with her grand-mother's clock and a trio of willowware plates with matching teapot.

Ada's recollection was of a warm spring afternoon when Christopher had just turned seven and they went together to buy a birthday gift for Amelia, who was soon to be seven and, like Christopher, was in the first grade. Since Ada and Christopher were equally anxious to please Amelia, it was assumed by Ada that the choice of a suitable gift would be no less difficult for him than it promised to be for her, all things con-sidered. And one of the things to be considered, cer-tainly, was a resemblance between Amelia and the lit-tle girl Ada had been.

In thirty years, Ada supposed, little girls had changed a bit. Visible signs of such changes, however, were few and far between. As a matter of fact, the only difference that Ada could see — between the little girl that she had been and the little girl Amelia now ap-peared to be — was in the way their braids were worn. Ada's braids had been wound about her head and secured with pins, and the psychological effect of having worn a crown of braids in childhood was so nearly permanent that, although her braids had been shingled away twenty years ago, she momentarily could feel their weight upon her head. What was perhaps more unfortunate, her behavior occasionally indicated a marked imbalance between timidity and boldness. Nor was it, she thought, an individual aberration. All of the women of her acquaintance who had ever worn a crown of braids in childhood had this fault — a fault that Amelia, whose braids were free of pins, never would have.

With this pleasant picture of Amelia in mind, Ada could see the difficulty of choosing a gift even more clearly than she did when she and Christopher had entered the shop. Naturally, the gift should be one that Ada, at the age of six, would have wanted.

"A pony would be nice," she said, pointing to a small ceramic replica of a horse. "Don't you think so?"

"I'll take this," Christopher said, taking the clay facsimile of a little boy with wings from one of the shelves. "Do you like it?"

"Amelia will love him, I'm sure."

When Christopher surprised her — and his decision to take a miniature representation of himself as a birthday gift to Amelia was surprising — Ada ordinarily tried to conceal her astonishment. It was, she supposed, less than honest to do this, but kinder to Christopher's pride. At the age of seven, after all, what can we give to the one we love but ourselves?

Later, when Ada and Christopher were at home, he unwrapped the gift and held it in both hands as he might have held a wounded bird to gauge its chances for survival. Then he set the figurine on top of the bookcase and went out of doors to bounce a ball against the house.

It seemed to Ada, standing alone and face to face with the tiny figure, that its face had the precise look Christopher's had when he was doing his homework. Its attire, too — a red stocking cap pulled low on the taut head, a snug green pullover, and faded blue jeans — was so familiar that she could not help smiling. It was the male stance, however — the arms held high and apart in a gesture that implied a readiness to give, or take, whatever the wide eyes wanted — that gave life to the clay. Behind one foot, in a clump of sod, a single flower bloomed, as though the artist, knowing how much vitality his creation enclosed, had tethered one foot to the ground to prevent its taking to the air on the pair of polka-dotted wings he should not have given to such a small boy.

Still smiling when Christopher came indoors from playing, Ada said, "If I had seen that little boy first, I'd have bought him for myself."

"But Mother, he's not a boy," Christopher said. "He's an elf."

Even more surprisingly, on the afternoon of Amelia's party he left the elf at home and took a gift of candy instead.

Twenty years later — when Christopher was visiting Ada with Joan and their children — the figurine fell, and a piece of that clump of sod from which a single flower grew had to be reset with Elmer's glue.

This, after all that had happened in those twenty years — a world war and the deaths of her parents, in addition to her husband's daily confrontations with the bored, and boring, aspects of public service as a teacher of both mathematics and Christian conduct — seemed to Ada to have been a minor mishap of the sort she could accept without making an effort to undo it.

Christopher, on the other hand, had fetched a bottle of glue from her desk and, matching his facial expression to the figurine's sober look, mended the damaged sod.

So, in good health and high spirits, the little elf had survived his fall and subsequent removal from the fireplace mantel to his present position of honor among the treasured relics on the kitchen shelf. He was over forty years old. And Ada was going to be seventy in June.

Now it was that time in May when the Persian yellow roses bloom; Ada, having mowed the lawn, had expected to sit on the terrace with her handsome collie and smell the roses. The arrival of visitors in a massive and unfamiliar station wagon was therefore inopportune, if not quite unwelcome. She knew — more exactly, she had known — several persons who would have been happy to share a terrace bench and the roses with her. But they were dead, and the occupants of the station wagon — a fair-haired woman and a little boy — in no way resembled them. They were what Ada's father might have called "intruders."

"Hi," Ada said in the crisp greeting her granddaughters often used.

"You are Mrs. Gibson, aren't you?" the woman said, joining Ada on the terrace.

"Yes."

Then, standing close, the woman said, "This is my son Reuben."

Reuben, at this, had not moved closer but continued to stand at a discreet distance from his mother and Ada. His head was held high and his carriage suggested both curiosity and condescension.

"But do I know you?" Ada said.

"I'm Mrs. Neff. We met last week at the store. Don't you remember?"

"Oh, yes, of course I do." And it was true that Ada had not only met this woman but had had an awkward conversation with her as she was leaving the store.

"Your husband was such a nice man," Mrs. Neff

said, smiling so broadly that her eyes were closed by the effort.

"He was an interesting man," Ada answered, feeling too full of admiration for Mrs. Neff's teeth to smile.

Conversations with young women — and, invariably, they were young — who for reasons that Ada did not understand seemed to think it was their duty to remind her of Marty's virtues had become, in the years since his death, as familiar as her own arthritic thumbs. It was as though they imagined that the sound of their voices could comfort her the way Marty's voice had.

"He always admired my little girl's dress," Mrs. Neff said.

"Mr. Gibson admired little girls. And big ones, too . . ." It was hardly necessary, since Mrs. Neff was blond and, obviously, concerned with other matters, to tell her that Marty preferred brunettes.

"Sometimes he gave money to my boys."

"Really?" Ada said, with a smile intended for Reuben.

Reuben gave no sign — or had the lid of one eye lowered in the ghost of a wink? — that he shared his mother's memories of Marty's openhandedness.

Mrs. Neff, who was smiling again, said, "I have two boys. Reuben is the older one. Adam is younger." She paused before carrying her thought forward. "And he wants to be with you."

"Why?"

"He pities you and doesn't want you to be alone."

Was it possible, Ada wondered, that she'd heard the words she seemed to have heard? When she was Reuben's age, small boys, from time to time, had demonstrated their willingness to be with her, and her parents withheld their approval. But neither the boys nor her parents had considered the fact that she was alone a sufficient cause for pity. She had been fortunate in her parents, her husband, and her son — too fortunate, perhaps, to have learned to face the hard facts that develop ingenuity and endurance in a woman. But, whatever the blessings of her life had been, it never was necessary to use, either in speaking of her own condition or the plight of her acquaintances, the word Mrs. Neff used. Pity, like gifts of money and advice, required care in the giving, a care that Ada presently was herself too surprised to give.

In Reuben's unsmiling face there was, Ada thought, a glimmer of amusement. Surely it was not pity that she saw there.

"It is your younger son who pities me?"

"Yes, Adam is sensitive."

Mrs. Neff waited then, as she might have waited in midstream to regain her balance while deciding which one of the slippery stones would carry her forward with the least risk of falling. Ada, reminded of Christopher in levitation, said, "Boys *are* sensitive."

"Adam thinks that you should not be alone." And, once again, Mrs. Neff smiled so broadly that her eyes were closed.

"What do you think I should pay Adam — for being with me?"

"He wants to be with you."

"Even so, he must be paid. Time is money, you know."

"Whatever you can give him," Adam's mother said.

"Will fifty cents an hour be enough, do you think?"

After a perceptible pause, in which Mrs. Neff again seemed to be balancing her weight on a moss-grown stone in midstream, she said, "Yes. It's not good for boys to be playing all the time."

"Wouldn't it be better," Ada asked, "for them to play all the time than to be men who went to their graves without ever knowing how to play? You want your boys to be boys, don't you?"

Mrs. Neff then — as though she had not heard Ada's question — bent both of her well-rounded arms at the elbow and shook a pair of neat fists at the amber sky. It was a gesture that Ada, neither before nor after her crown of braids was shingled away, had ever performed. Without lowering her arms, Mrs. Neff said, "I am young and you — when summer comes and the sun is hot — will need help."

"How soon do you think that will happen?

While it was true that every day had its unexpected happenings, Ada did not yet foresee the day when the sun might be too hot for her to follow her own inclinations without help. It was, however, as Mrs. Neff had said, a possibility.

And Reuben, smiling for the first time since his arrival, said, "School will be over the tenth of June."

"Shall we wait and see how I feel when school is over?" Ada said.

Later, when Reuben and his mother were gone, Ada went to smell the roses and found that their petals already were falling. It was as though that moment of the year — the time when the tight buds opened wide to turn an awkward mass of thorns into a garland of lemon-colored rosettes — had come and gone when Mrs. Neff shook her fists at the gentle sky.

The next morning, Ada made an appointment to talk with Dr. Schultz about the depressing prospect of spending what, for all she knew, might be the rest of her life with Reuben and Adam Neff.

She imagined that if the doctor knew the lengths to which Mrs. Neff had gone to create a sense of obligation in Ada's mind, he would read her blood pressure and say, as from time to time he did, "Ada, your blood pressure is up today. My advice is to avoid irritating situations."

Instead of saying that, however, he gave her a cheerful pat on the arm from which he had just removed the pressure bandage and said, "That's good. Your pressure was down. What have you been doing?"

"Things I like to do — for the most part. What I need is more time. I'll soon be seventy years old, you know."

"There are people younger than you are who are less well than you. I see them every day," Dr. Schultz said, looking thoughtful.

"I see them, too. But I had to talk to you about Mrs. Neff. Do you know her?"

"Yes."

"She believes that I will need one or both of her boys to be with me when school is out. And I doubt it very much. What's more, I had planned to enjoy myself this summer."

"How old are the Neff boys?" Dr. Schultz did not laugh the way he often did when, under the spell of his healing powers, she had made a witty comment.

"Mrs. Neff didn't say. The one I've seen wasn't very big."

"Their mother is less financially secure than you

are." The doctor's eyes seemed to be full of tears and his voice was gentle.

"But I was looking forward to being completely selfish and busy with my own ideas. The Neff boys are strangers to me. You know the saying, 'In order to know a man you must have known his grandfather'?"

"They're not men. They're little boys. I know that because I used to be their doctor."

"Would it shock you if I said that I don't want to be with little boys?"

"No."

"I'm sorry," Ada said, getting up and smiling down at the man whose willingness to heal others embraced both Mrs. Neff and herself. "I'll go now."

"Mrs. Gibson?"

"Yes, Dr. Schultz?"

"It might be nicer than you expect — to give the Neff boys a chance."

When Adam Neff came to be with Ada, she saw that his smile was more ingenuous than his mother's and less inward than Reuben's.

The long gray eyes, Nordic complexion, and ivory-tinted teeth were so nearly identical with those features in the faces of Reuben and his mother that Ada wondered how Mrs. Neff had achieved this double duplication of herself. In other words, how many nondominant traits did fathers of Mr. Neff's generation have?

Ada wondered, too, how it happened that Adam, disregarding her suggestion that it would be unnecessary for him to come to be with her on rainy days, had arrived in a downpour. Even more difficult for Ada to understand was how Adam, on arrival, had seized the doorknob — while her collie stood at attention on the doormat — and was bitten. After which she, all shame and contrition, drove Adam to his mother's house, and told her to have the wound treated without delay by Dr. Schultz.

"I'll pay for the call," Ada said.

"We don't go to Dr. Schultz anymore." Mrs. Neff smiled, then, with her eyes closed, and said, "The dog is all right, isn't he?"

"Yes. The dog is all right. But I'm concerned about Adam."

Whereupon Adam, still holding the dollar Ada had paid him for the time it had taken her collie to bite him, said, "I think you should have that dog put to sleep."

"No," Ada said. "It's his job to watch my house."

"You should have a friendlier dog."

And Ada, now neither contrite nor ashamed, said, "No, I don't think that I should have a friendlier dog. I need this one."

It was true, as Marty often had said during those years when he was a teacher, "The hardest thing in the world is to help people."

The next day, Adam was driven by his mother to be with Ada, and when they were alone he said, "My mother will be pleased with me if I can hold this job."

"How old are you?"

"Eight. I'll be nine in September. That's Virgo, you know."

"I'm Gemini and my granddaughters are coming to spend my birthday with me."

"Are they bigger than I am?"

"Yes, they're *big* girls." Ada did not think it necessary to say that they were older than he and, almost certainly, as large as they ever would be.

"Then I won't come to work until they've gone home."

"All right. I'll tell you when they've gone."

"Don't forget. I must work because my mother got a divorce."

It would have been easy for her to have said, "I'm sorry." But looking into Adam's angry little-boy face, she smiled, and said, "What do you want for your birthday — when you are nine?"

"I want to go to the cemetery where Mr. Gibson is buried."

"We'll go there together on your birthday," Ada

said, handing him a pair of grass shears. "And now we'll go to work."

A week later, when Christopher telephoned, the tone of his voice was less confident than it had been on that spring afternoon when he chose — from the innumerable treasures of their favorite gift shop — an elf for Amelia. It was, in fact, tentative to the verge of being outrightly apologetic when he spoke of visiting her.

The banter with which his telephone calls usually began seemed to be forced and had given way at once to a serious estimate of the number of guests she might expect.

"The children are not as easy to organize as they once were," he said. "The girls want to come. And Jude, too. But there is a dance on Saturday night. Bruce, you know, has a summer job."

"I know," Ada said.

"So I'll be coming with the girls. How long do you think you can put up with us?"

"As long as you can put up with me, I imagine."

"In that case, we'll be there on the day before your birthday and leave on the following day."

"Wonderful."

"What shall we bring — for the celebration?"

"Yourselves. I don't need anything else."

"Let us know if you change your mind."

"I'll do that."

"Goodbye, then, until we see you."

"Have a safe trip," she said.

The voice she had heard was Christopher's with a quality that she associated with age. When well-meaning friends said, "If you feel well, your age doesn't matter," they were trying to be kind and talking nonsense. The truth was that age does matter. With this thought in mind, Ada returned to the chore that Christopher's call had interrupted and, after mixing the dry cat food with sardines and water, went to the porch, where a number of cats were waiting to be fed.

The number of cats — mostly black with white feet and bizarre facial markings of white — was ten. An equal number, unless a new set of kittens was born in the night, waited for Ada in the barn. And there had been a time, long ago, when she wished that God, in His mercy, would take the cats from her care into His own. But even though a virus, at the time, was rampant in her neighborhood and whole families of cats had succumbed, her own pride — clear-eyed and glossy — continued to increase in numbers until Marty, foreseeing a time when his pension (in its entirety) might be spent for cat food, asked those men who habitually hunted in the nearby woods — now and then at their convenience — to hunt cats. Yet all had refused and, to a man, said, "Oh no, I couldn't shoot Ada's cats." It was as if these neighbors who could, without qualms of any kind, shoot a rabbit, a doe, or a dog afield on a friendly call had joined one of the ancient cults of cat worshippers.

Nor was her own thinking, when it turned to the cats, entirely logical. There had been kittens in many of those snapshots taken by her when she was young and her Brownie new. Other kittens, lost to the photographic record, still lived — soft, warm, and amusing — among memories that, on the whole, were neither warm nor amusing. But, remembering those kittens, was it necessary for her to feed twenty mature cats now?

There were, among her acquaintances, those who repeatedly said, "Ada, all you have to do to be rid of your cats is to stop feeding them."

Ada's answer to this advice was a question that, even while she asked it, brought tears to her eyes. "Have you ever seen a cat that is starving to death?"

"No. Cats can catch birds and mice."

"While they are young and strong. Eventually malnutrition makes them less predatory and they die. It wouldn't be fair to the cats — or my neighbors — to stop feeding them. Don't you understand?"

But of course they did not. Otherwise they never would have told her to stop feeding the cats.

Waiting now for Ada to set the wide dish of mixed feed on the porch floor, Tallulah and Whiskey — a pair of middle-aged sisters whose young invariably were born in the woods and only when ambulatory came to the porch — raised their heads and opened their mouths to make what, in less patient animals, would have been a complaint.

"An unanswered prayer is a small price to pay for a pair of such grace and gentility," Ada thought, putting down the dish. "A summer without kittens would be dull as a spring without swallows."

Tallulah's three kittens then joined her for breakfast while Whiskey, that aunt who sometimes suckled them when their mother was detained in the fields, blinked and licked her lips in silent approval.

True to his promise, Christopher and Ada's grand-daughters arrived on the day before her birthday.

Both of the girls had been ruddy, round-faced babies and, though teenagers now, continued to be ruddy and round-faced. And when anyone, on meeting them for the first time, told Ada how greatly they resembled her, she always smiled and said, "Do you really think so?"

To Ada their likeness to the girl she had been was negligible. It was, now that she saw them, difficult for her to believe that Christopher was their father. They seemed to belong completely to Joan. More strangely still, there was an urgency about their need to shed their clothes and lie in the sun that — in spite of the fact that Christopher when a teenager had said, "Mother, it's not easy to shock you" — shocked her. Roommates in her college days had thought it necessary to dress and undress in their clothes closets. Nor had they done this because they could foresee the time when their skins would be irreparably damaged by the sun's actinic rays. The truth, quite simply, was that, like Adam in the Garden of Eden, they were "afraid." In short, girls had changed since she was a girl.

On the morning of Ada's birthday, Molly and Sarah — bikini-clad and barefoot — picked berries in a bramble patch and baked a perfect pie, speaking to each other in voices so musical that Ada, hearing them, felt pure joy. Later, they washed their long brown hair with herbal shampoo and brushed it dry.

So the morning of Ada's birthday was spent and, when it was nearly noon, the girls watched, with their father, as Ada opened her presents. A sensation of warmth seemed to radiate from the bright tissues, and all of the cards said, "To Mom-mom with much love." The string of blue beads was from Joan and the matching earrings were from Sarah. Molly's gift was an etching and Jude's an enlarged and moody photograph of a coneflower growing on the hillock beside the house where they now lived. Bruce, fully aware that she would accept his summer job as a token of his affection, had sent no gift. A pair of camel bells conveyed Christopher's congratulations.

"You told me not to bring anything," Christopher said, in the odd way he had spoken to her on the telephone.

"I meant what I said and couldn't be more pleased. Thank you."

"You're very welcome. I wish we could have brought you something more suitable for a birthday of such importance."

"A visit was what I needed — from you and my granddaughters."

Then, in a voice so gentle that it scarcely could be heard, he said, "There is something you should know, Mother."

"Is it that I'm not really seventy years old today?"

"Don't you like being seventy years old?"

"I'm not sure that I do."

"I was going to tell you that I have a small apartment in the city and could take a larger one, if you want to come and live there."

"I would like that. But who would live here with the cats?"

"What I'm trying to say is this. I'm leaving Joan."

"How can you? What will become of the boys?"

"I'm worried about the boys — Jude, especially."

"Do you have to leave them?"

"There are ways of getting a man to leave."

"And a way of staying. I did."

"Girls are not like boys, Mother."

At these words, Ada's grandmother's clock began to strike and, when Ada had counted to twelve, she said, "The clock's tired. I forgot to wind it. Poor thing."

Ada's mother had habitually approached the clock as she approached those older members of the family to whom deference, or affection, belonged, and had instructed her daughter to do the same. And now, standing on one of the kitchen chairs, Ada respectfully took the clock's big brass key in hand while an echo of her mother's voice whispered, "You should be sure, Ada, to give the same number of turns on both sides. One, two. One, two. Until you can't turn it again." Occasionally, when Ada's mother had neglected to wind the clock, time stood still, and Ada's father, looking into its bland face, had threatened to go to the local tavern for the meal he had expected to find ready on his own table. Below the kitchen shelf, Marty's electric clock still hung from the wall, setting the pace for her grandmother's clock until a power failure made it necessary for Ada to turn its hands to the time that her grandmother's clock said it was.

Now, having turned the hands of her grand-mother's clock to the time indicated by the electric clock and returned the key to its place behind the briskly swinging pendulum, she gently closed the clock's door and stepped from the chair to see that Christopher, in the next room, had begun to clean his rifle.

"I thought that, while I'm here, you might want me to shoot a few cats."

"Yes, I do. But I want, even more than that, to know why you are abandoning your children."

"It's not easy to say. I'd rather not talk about it."

"I know. And I'd rather not know."

Somewhat too tightly wound now, the old clock struck the half hour with so much noisy nonchalance that Christopher, looking up from the love seat where he was cleaning his rifle, said, "I'll bet that clock knows everything." And his voice was angry — as the voices of his father and grandfather were whenever they spoke of her grandmother's clock.

"Your father is teasing us, I think," Ada said, look-ing at the girls and wondering if, in reality, her smile ever had been as beguiling as the smiles being ex-changed by her granddaughters.

"Yes, Mom-mom. Uncle Christopher is teasing," Molly said.

Girls of Ada's generation rarely had referred to their

father as "uncle." Yet, in a household where the grandmother's clock knew everything, Ada doubted if it would be useful to turn its hands to another time than the one to which they now were pointing.

"No, Mother," Christopher said, "the time has come when I must do something for the boy I used to be."

"And what can I do for him? He was such a good boy."

"Just love us all."

Christopher's answer was so surprising that Ada could not speak. It was almost as though after thirty-five years they had returned to their favorite gift shop in the week before Amelia's birthday. The time then was spring. The time now was summer and the birthday Ada's. And again she was speechless while making a judgment in favor of a decision Christopher had made for the boy he was.

Later, perhaps, she would love them all. Until then, it was good to know that boys — unlike girls — had not changed.

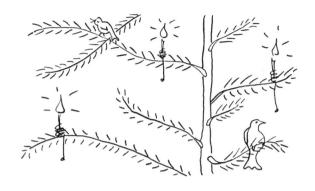

The Papier-Mâché
Santa Claus

THE TALL CEDAR, with its sweet smell and long
strings of tinsel, was as exciting as a first Christmas
tree could have been expected to be. There was a bell
quietly ringing from the tip of the tree that curved
down from the ceiling, and Ada's mother had set a
papier-mâché Santa Claus on the floor under the tree.
A chunk of chestnut wood crackled in the big stove
and sunshine filled the east window and the bird that
often sang in her heart was singing when her grandfather said, "Ada, there is no Santa Claus."

He looked so solemn that she knew he was trying
to be kind. Old people try to protect us from evil, she
thought, and must be forgiven for saying so much that
we do not need to hear. Certainly it had been unneces-

sary for her grandfather to say there is no Santa Claus. Even if she had not always known it, there would have been no need for him to tell her. When a bird sings in your heart and your father has cut a cedar tree for the house, a papier-mâché Santa Claus will do.

Sitting on the striped carpet beside the Santa Claus, Ada took a long look at him. His coat was sky blue and sparkled with artificial snow. His face was pale and peaked, like her mother's, not red and fat like her father's or the pictured faces of Santa Claus. Nor was this the face of a kind man who sometimes picked her up without warning and laughed when he said, "I only wanted to know if I could lift you." This was a sober, thoughtful man — and handsome.

Now her grandfather, who long ago must have been both sober and handsome, if not thoughtful, sat in his big rocking chair beside the stove, eating apple scrapings with a spoon. With her back to the stove, she took a deep breath of the fragrance of apple and forgave him for having said there is no Santa Claus. She understood that it was his way of asking her not to cry when she saw that Christmas trees in other houses had heaps and heaps of gifts under them.

When her son and only child was five years old, Ada set the papier-mâché Santa Claus under an Austrian pine for which she had paid the tree grower two dollars. The carpet was a soft gray broadloom, and Christopher was sitting beside the track on which a sky-blue Lionel train ran beneath the tree. Ada and Marty had just been arguing about whether or not she should have spent two dollars for the tree. What Christopher thought while the train travelled through a monk's-cloth landscape uninhabited except for the Santa Claus he did not say. When his father, looking very red in the face, said, "Ada, it is time you learned that there is no Santa Claus," it seemed as though Christopher had not heard him.

Since Christopher smiled as he sent the blue train whistling on its circuitous course beneath the Austrian pine, Ada assumed that the bird she had heard singing in her heart beside a cedar tree thirty years earlier now sang in his heart, and an hour later, when a boy with whom Christopher occasionally played paid them a Christmas call and asked, "Is that all you got?" she thought the question shockingly rude. The little blue train jumped its track just then, and Christopher, still smiling, replaced it without a word.

After breakfast, when Marty had gone to work, Christopher backed his car across the frozen lawn and Ada smiled at her daughter-in-law, Joan, and said, "This is

Epiphany." Both her smile and the words were keep-sakes her father often had used to remind her of time's passage, and Ada was happy to recall them now.

Joan held a string of yellow beads she had just found on the carpet in the shadow of the piano bench and her face was flushed, the way it was when she col-lected the children's belongings prior to their depar-ture. Once, a doll forgotten, Christopher had backed away from the turnpike entrance and returned. That was when Molly had been an only child. Now that there were three children, Joan's experience in shep-herding toys and clothing into the little blue car had made her so expert that an oversight rarely occurred. Nor did Ada, in reality, hope for one. It was a day for moving away from the past. The sky was a lovely shade of green, and cloudless.

As though to the magic of a green and cloudless sky one of her father's sayings must be added to assure them of the day's pleasant portent, Ada went outdoors and repeated the announcement she had made to Joan. "This, Christopher, is Epiphany."

"Really, Mother?" Christopher's eyes widened in a sober stare to let her know that he remembered his grandfather's habit of calling their attention to the passage of time. "Do you think Epiphany is a good day for us to be leaving?"

"The weather will be good all the way."

"Are you sorry that Christmas is over and we have to leave?"

"Christmas isn't over. This is Epiphany."

"Yes, I know. You've told me."

At this they laughed, suddenly and savagely, the way Molly and Bruce, downstairs before breakfast, had laughed when they saw a wood fire dancing in the fireplace. Then, with the sound of their laughter, the air had turned to water and those things which tend to be airborne — echoes of long-dead voices, and lint; even objects as substantial as the piano and her own stout body — floated. The miracle had lasted but a moment and Ada supposed it was one of the sensations a woman invariably experiences when her grandchildren are laughing. Now, however, while she watched Christopher fit a puzzle of cartons and suitcases into the car's trunk, she again felt the odd buoyancy and said, "How nice it must be to put everything where it really fits."

"I don't know when we'll come again. It's a long trip."

His words rustled in the cold air and sounded like those strips of glazed paper she sometimes used to pack a fragile gift.

"I know it," she said. "You've come a long way."

"Oh, do you think so?"

"Everyone does. We are very proud of you."

"Pride isn't Christian, you know."

Had he intended this gentle reproof to be taken seriously, Ada thought, he would not have raised his eyebrows and smiled as if her play on words had been a piece of warm apple pie.

"If true, that's the tragic flaw of Christianity," she said.

Without answering, Christopher looked away to the east; in profile, he reminded her of the boy who, in another time of their lives, when both were believed to be too young to wear the toga virilis in her father's house, had said, "Mother, you can't help me anymore. I'm grateful for the help you've given me. But you can't help me anymore. You must stop trying."

Into the stillness that followed Christopher's words then she had breathed the little white lie that had been one of her conversational habits. "I know. I know."

But how could she have known that so harsh a prohibition was, in reality, a simple statement of the truth? In the years that followed, it had been true, and in the years to come it almost certainly would be. The time of Christopher's next visit, however, was uncertain and must remain so. She could accept its uncertainty as easily as, at the age of six, she had accepted the solitary presence of the papier-mâché Santa Claus under her Christmas tree.

When Joan thanked her for a lovely visit and the doors of the car were buttoned tight, Ada went into the house and stood beside one of the windows that overlooked the road to the turnpike. Ordinarily, the Christmas season brought snow. But since the ground was bare, a spindrift of dust followed the little blue car down the road and across a short stretch of level ground that Ada's mother had called "the flat" to the edge of Jackson's hill. Here the car abruptly dropped from sight and the dust drifted in a small sienna cloud above a field of winter wheat.

Then, facing the room and a small blue spruce that she had cut from one of her own plantings of nursery stock, Ada sat in her favorite chair. Among the tree's sparse decorations she had set a titmouse nest with a clutch of tinsel beads. Assorted animals from the world of Walt Disney waited in a wistful *attroupement* where formerly the papier-mâché Santa Claus had stood.

In the space around her chair and the Christmas tree the spirits of her lately departed guests still moved, very much as their bodies had moved during their visit. Molly still extended a cupless acorn to Ada and asked, "Mom-mom, what is it? What is it? I found it under that big tree in the woods." Bruce — who had just learned to walk alone — and his mother continued to circle the room in parallel orbits, each so quietly busy that Ada, who seldom could combine busyness with silence, had watched in amazement. The baby, Jude, was asleep in his carry cot and had not begun to cry until Christopher settled the portable bed into the car's back seat and said, "I don't know when we'll come again. It's a long way to bring little children."

Now that she thought of Christopher's words, it occurred to her that sometimes when she had felt melancholy her father said, "Ada, you mustn't let your imagination run away with you." He rarely had been tactless to the point of saying more than that, yet his implication plainly was that a person who gave a free rein to her imagination might be stranded for life in the land of whimsy. Since neither he nor any of the other members of her family had given a free rein to their imaginations, it was almost certain that her stay in the land of whimsy would be a lonely one and therefore to be avoided at all costs. So it was that her survival began to depend more and more on using her father's formula for converting hindsight, foresight, and insight into wit that in her conversation — as it had in her father's — might pass for wisdom. Moreover, it now seemed to Ada that she had seen her father become a wise man just as surely as, in the seven years since his death, Christopher, his grandson and namesake, had become a well-known illustrator of children's books. At the same time, it seemed as though, along with the old house and its furniture, she had inherited the responsibility of pretending to be more wise than, in reality, she was.

But if, considering her own fundamental foolishness, the notion that she could follow in her father's footsteps was presumptuous, it was an idea so charged with enchantment that Ada could not resist it.

Beside her chair in the library of the big house, a rose-colored hibiscus was blooming in a wooden tub. It was both lovely and unreal in the special way that a tree in full bloom in December often is, and Ada was thrilled by the sight.

More than that, the presence of *Hibiscus rosa-sinensis* in bloom for the winter holidays was — as were the Matisse above the fireplace and a recently bought *Dictionary of the English Language* by Samuel Johnson — indicative of the long way she had come. Planes, by reducing the travel time, tended to be misleading. But the distance between Christopher's home and her own had not lessened in the years since Jude was a baby and Molly had found an acorn under a big tree. The distances between people and places rarely changed. The belief that they could be shortened by an effort of the will was one of the many ways she had been tempted to let her imagination run away with her. Thanks to her father's advice, however, she had not yielded to that temptation.

Beyond the hibiscus, books lined the wall and, having taken one at random from its shelf, she read that "for the ancient Greeks, potted plants were tokens of yearly rebirth."

Even without a picture of Eros giving a bunch of seedlings to a young female who, presumably, was expecting to attend a celebration of Adonic rites, Ada almost certainly would have been reminded of Marty — Marty, who happily had lived long enough to see Joan and Christopher at home in this handsome house.

When, during their long premarital acquaintance, had Marty said, "We must have a son — like you"? Having stated this paradox, he had smiled the gentle smile that he might have smiled seeing her beside the blooming hibiscus. It was the smile she missed now and would miss for as long as she lived. It was the smile that had filled Marty's eyes whenever they spoke of Christopher.

Snow had fallen during the early morning and clung to every limb and ledge so that, incredibly, the dainty twigs of a smoke tree close to the front door supported miniature skyscrapers of snow.

At the age of six, Ada had attended a school where

the teacher, whenever it was snowing, invited his pupils to join him in singing a hymn of praise in which the words "snow, snow, beautiful snow" were repeated again and again until the wonder that had befallen them became more nearly endurable. Unfortunately, she could not remember the tune, and instead of singing it she called attention to the snow in the way that her father habitually had called everyone's attention to the passage of time.

Later, Molly announced to Ada that the time to open their gifts had come, and she joined the others in the big room where a mountain of presents shone from the shade of the Christmas tree. When all of the packages had been opened and admired and their wrappings taken away, Jude and Sarah, the two youngest of her grandchildren, under Joan's direction lit the candles on a balsam fir that Bruce had cut and brought from the hill beyond the house. The tree's top touched the ceiling and its branches held both candles and birds.

When it was time for Ada to leave, she said, "This is the nicest Christmas I've ever had."

At this, Joan laughed and raised her eyebrows, while Christopher — like his mother a holiday guest in the lovely house — looked on, a sober, thoughtful man in a blue coat.

A Week of Prayer

ON A SUNDAY in October, Ada Gibson's was among
the names of those whom Pastor Pruitt prayed for
and asked the congregation to remember in prayer
throughout the following week. The pastor, beaming,
held her hand a second longer than usual after the
service and said, "You will have a good week."

"But of course," Ada said. "I know that."

Pastor Pruitt's handclasp tightened, as though to
express even more forcibly their acknowledged conviction that the week ahead of Ada would be as good
as the enjoined prayers of his congregation could
make it, and she, smiling the girlish smile that somehow had survived both Marty's death and the divorce
of their son, Christopher, withdrew her hand from
the pastor's warm embrace to take a double grip on her

handbag before she began to edge her way through the crowd that now thronged the narthex. Her smile, no longer girlish, had become indicative more of perseverance than of pleasure.

Had Marty been with her, the question that entered her mind would have been answered hours ago. Even before the church service began, he would have foreseen what she should do once it was over. Because of his foresight in such small matters of Christian deportment, Marty had enjoyed a considerable reputation for courtesy, and Ada, relieved of the obligation to make those choices upon which a reputation for courtesy depends, had been free to meditate on the grosser aspects of humanity.

Small talk, too, had been a gift of Marty's that she now needed and, regrettably, lacked. It was as though, after preparing her for the excitement she had found in driving his nimble-footed small car, he had said to himself, "That is enough for Ada to know." And, indeed, her experience in the years since his death had proven him right. The main thing was being able to drive his car. When not driving, a widow smiled and kept a two-handed hold on her purse.

The brass handle of the church door was almost within reach when a woman, clinging to the arm of her husband, said, "There goes Mrs. Gibson, looking like she's in another world."

Marty would have seized the hand of the mute husband and congratulated him on his wife's fine appearance and thereby put a smile on his face, if not on the faces of all who had heard her. Later, driving home, he might have said, "Ada, you can expect to have your feelings hurt when you are older. That's the price we pay for a long life."

Still smiling and still holding her handbag in both hands, she remained silent. Ada could think of no suitable rejoinder now. The truth was that she had been in another world — that world she once shared with Marty and Christopher.

When the door of the church was closed behind her at long last, she stopped for a moment to savor the euphoria of standing alone on the upper stone of the wide stairway that led ever so gently into the world of the unchurched. It was here that her father's spirit sometimes joined her own in celebration of the fact, recognized by them both, that Christianity and the rubbing together of one pair of elbows with innumerable others, known commonly by the name of "fellowship," are not the same thing.

The stone on which she stood was one her father had helped wheel into place when the church was built and he was a young and loose-jointed lad, and it was here that she could feel his blessing.

Feeling it now, she remembered the way he had looked when he said, "We must carry our own hides to market. Nobody can do that for us."

The analogy was crude and contrary to many current practices. Yet how did one escape the truth of one's own singularity? At least her father's words gave her the answer to what she should do next; with the pride that comes from carrying one's own hide Ada drove the eight lovely country miles to her favorite restaurant.

"Welcome to the Madison Inn," the waitress said. "My name is Elaine and it will be my pleasure to serve you. Will you be having the smorgasbord today?"

"Yes. Thank you."

"Do you like this table?"

"Oh, yes. That will be fine."

Then, since the smorgasbord was not quite ready, Ada waited by a window overlooking the highway while a procession of high-stepping bay horses attached to Amish buggies trotted past the inn and the little church where George Washington — one time, for certain — had stopped on his way to a stay with General Hand at Rockford. When the buggies were out of sight and the quick beat of the horses' feet on the macadam had faded away, Ada's eyes were filled with tears. Tears of astonished joy on account of the procession's survival — all reason to the contrary — and her own.

During the night, Ada woke with a start. Had an automobile door slammed nearby in the road, or was it the report of a deer rifle in the woods west of the house? In any event, what could she do now? She would go to sleep and expect all to be well in the morning. With the world so full of "fellowship," it was natural for nights to be noisy.

When Ada got out of bed several hours later and went to a window, she saw Venus and a dainty slice of the moon in a cloudless sky — nothing more. "Thank you, Heavenly Father," she said, "for this sight."

In midmorning, having gone to fetch the milk from the small metal bin where the milkman had left it, she discovered that the mailbox was missing from the cedar post where Marty, with her help, had fastened it. Such a thing could not have happened, and yet quite plainly her mailbox was not in the place where, for the last twelve years, it had been. After an immeasurable moment in which disbelief gave way to righteous indignation, Ada began to count the steps to be taken in order to receive a letter. Happily, it was Columbus Day, and there would be plenty of time to do what had to be done.

Her first step, after taking the milk to the house and asking for divine guidance, would be to drive from house to house to see whether her mailbox was at one of them. In the event that it was not, the second step would be to go to the local hardware store and buy another mailbox. The third and final step, having found either her own or a new one, would be to pray for the ability to anchor it on the post.

As it turned out, when Ada left the house, her purse and car keys in hand, a neighbor drove into view with her mailbox riding tandem on his tractor.

Ada felt too relieved to smile. "Where did you find my mailbox?" she asked.

"Where *our* mailbox usually is." He gave her a look as sober as her own surely was. "Ours was down at the Gordon place."

"What have we done to offend them?"

"Nothing."

"We set those rocks in the woods to keep out the pickup trucks."

"But we didn't have to do anything to make them move our mailboxes. That sort of thing happens all the time."

"So I've heard. And what can I do now to show how much I appreciate your bringing my mailbox back?"

"Do you think you could hold it steady while I nail it to the post?"

That done, they faced each other across the mailbox and exchanged broad smiles.

"Something much worse might have happened," Ada said, thinking of the way her collie — his advanced age and genteel breeding forgotten — threw himself at passing automobiles. "Duke is alive and well."

"Yes. A good many worse things might've happened," he said. "They could've taken a truckload of apples, instead of stopping when they'd stripped a few trees in the orchard. Like they did." Without saying another word, Ada's kind neighbor mounted the tractor and rode off in the direction of home.

On Tuesday just before noon, Ada looked up from a copy of *Let's Get Well,* by Adelle Davis, to find that a van of the sort retired schoolteachers frequently buy was parked in the driveway and a large man was walking somewhat unsteadily toward the house. Such men came to see how Ada was doing, whether because they had met Marty as members of the same union or as pupils who, in homage to Marty's touching attempts to teach them, had decided to follow in his footsteps. Their visits with Ada, naturally, lacked the warmth of meetings with Marty. Without a bedrock of shared experience, what could they say? Yet, remembering Marty, they came, and, remembering Marty, their conversation was agreeable — more often than not.

With the man who by this time had crossed her lawn and was standing at ease in the shade of the house, she certainly expected to have no verbal difficulty. Frank Nesbit, while never one of Marty's pupils, was a long-time teacher. At intervals of a year or two, he came to call on Ada, and the warm bluffness of manner that had marked his acquaintance with Marty was now transferred to her. After expressing her surprise and pleasure at seeing him, Ada asked the first question that occurred to her. "Where is Laura?"

"She's in the van. It's a new one."

"I can see that. It's very impressive."

"But you must see the inside. Everything is in it, excepting our grandchildren," he said as they walked toward the narrow steps leading into the shining vehicle. "We bought this for ourselves."

"Heaven and earth are only three short steps apart," Ada said. "But what if I should fall?"

"Watch your step."

"Perhaps you should go first?"

"No. I'll follow you. Just watch your step."

"I'll do that," she said, looking down and thinking how truly frail the little stairway seemed to be while she climbed it.

To Ada's surprise it sustained her weight, and in a second or two she was perched beside Laura on a narrow dais while Frank asked her to choose from several kinds of fruit on a plate. Then, as though this gesture of hospitality had put their relationship on a more intimate plane, he inquired about Christopher's health.

"He seems to be well."

"Don't you know?"

"Not really. His friends tell me that he is looking well and I wouldn't think of questioning their judgment. Christopher himself seldom complains of illness."

"But is he still working?"

"Yes."

"What about his divorce?"

"What is there to say about a divorce?"

Laura interrupted her husband at this point to say, " 'Good riddance.' That's what we said when Jack got his second wife. She's exactly right for us. She's like we are. The first one was too smart for Jack — and us. We're all much happier since the divorce."

"The children, too?"

"Yes, the children, too."

"That's hard for me to believe."

"You must learn to say good riddance, the way we did. It's as simple as that," Laura said, showing her handsome teeth and looking sideways at Ada.

"Oh no, I couldn't say that. It's not the truth."

"But we might as well accept it until the truth comes along."

"In a way, I have accepted it. But that's not the same as saying good riddance."

Marty's old friend, having passed a plum to Ada, sat

on one of the narrow benches with which the van seemed well supplied, got out a camera, and took a snapshot of her face in profile. At close range, his aura lacked the geniality that, as they had walked together across the lawn, suggested a friendliness beyond the curiosity ordinarily evident in the visits of those retired teachers Marty had known. Ada wondered whether his purpose in stopping was to add to his collection of candid pictures another snapshot of two formerly handsome women seated cheek by jowl in a new van, or whether she had heard in his quizzing of her a faint echo of the true concern an earnest teacher, when closeted with an indifferent pupil, must feel. Having always been an indifferent student, Ada smiled and came to the conclusion that his concern was genuine. His questions, after all, had been natural enough, since he and Marty had each been the father of one son only and since, besides, she had answered them many times before.

The interview ended, however, with a probing question so shocking that Ada at first doubted her hearing. "Do your grandchildren have a drug problem?"

"Only alcohol." The words had come to her as unexpectedly as the question, and now that she had spoken them were no less shocking.

Mr. Nesbit nodded. "In our schools, it is quite common for children to be drunk first thing in the morning," he said. Then, remembering that there were other calls to be made before he and his wife returned to that place where children were drunk all the day long, Marty's friend announced his departure. Before leaving, he again raised his camera and took a picture of the van's interior, including Ada and his wife.

Ada, returned to the earth, smiled at the retreating house on wheels. Aside from her lifelong addiction to coffee, she had no drug problems; nor was it likely that her grandchildren would become drug addicts. Problems with teachers, however, lasted a lifetime.

On Wednesday, Ada visited Elizabeth, an old friend who had not been a teacher and who was in frail health. This is not to say that their congeniality was based on these failures alone. They were both members of the Lutheran Church and had attended the same coeducational college, where each of them had married one of her classmates and converted him to Lutheranism.

Their conversation began, as their talks often did, with a discussion of death (their own) and the fact that, happily, both still lived.

"I'm not afraid to die," Elizabeth said. "I've been

close to death so many times. Yet I do enjoy this world and don't want to leave it."

"I know how you feel," Ada said. "It's a beautiful place to be, especially at this time of the year."

"Yes, I sat on the porch for a while today."

"When you tire of the sound of my voice, tell me and I'll leave."

"I'll tell you," Elizabeth said. "But the sound of your voice is not tiresome. Quite the contrary. Tell me, how are the children?"

Since Ada had no "children," it was understood that Elizabeth had meant to say "grandchildren."

"I don't know them well enough to say how they are."

"They're all talented, aren't they?"

"Yes, I think so. The only worrisome thing about grandchildren is that they tend to behave just like their grandparents at that age."

"I know." Shaken with laughter, Elizabeth pointed to the pastel of a handsome boy hanging on the wall behind an exquisitely hand-carved sofa. "That's exactly the way Bob is."

"I'll take your word." Ada was standing face to face with the portrait of the boy and hearing her father's voice: "We must always go home, Ada, before our welcome is worn out." Sound advice, she had learned on more than one occasion. So, wondering how threadbare the cordial welcome given to her by Elizabeth had become, she said, "Don't you want me to leave now?"

"Please wait till Bob comes home. He'll be here soon. You don't know how glad I am you came. You stimulate me, and I need that. There is so much I can't do I want to do that I'm often depressed."

Together, they circled the small room that was the world Elizabeth was loath to leave. In the years of her illness, the room had become both more elegant and more interesting in the way that a loved person, aware of the lover's need, tends to become more beautiful. A rose, full-blown and fragile in its crystal vase, seemed too near perfection to be real. Ada moved closer to it.

"That's the last rose of summer from an old and ne-glected bush," Elizabeth said. "I couldn't, you know, take care of my garden."

"It's beautiful," Ada said, looking down and hold-ing her breath, for surely such perfection could not endure even the mildest of air turbulence. "But then everything in this room is beautiful."

"I've never understood how it happened that the blues of that geode and the blue of our upholstery match. I didn't plan it. I didn't even buy the geode and the velvet together," Elizabeth said.

"Haven't you found that everything has a way of coming out right?" Before Elizabeth could answer, Bob came in. "Like having Bob arrive now," Ada said, "just as I really must be leaving."

"Don't go yet," Bob said.

He sounded so sincere that Ada sat down. "All right," she said, "shall I tell you the news about our old college friends?"

"Fine," Bob said.

"A lot of it is bad. I'll try not to tell you all of it."

But, while she was driving home, it seemed to Ada that everything she had told them was bad news and that she did, in the end, wear out her welcome.

On the day after her visit with Elizabeth and Bob, Ada received a telephone call from one of Christopher's former schoolmates.

"This is Christine West," she said. "Do you remember me?"

"Yes, certainly. How could I have forgotten you, Christine?"

"You'll think I'm crazy when you know why I'm calling."

"Try me."

"This really is fantastic."

"All the better."

"You won't think I'm crazy?"

"No, I won't. That's a promise."

"Christopher has been my prayer burden for a little more than a year now."

"He's been my prayer burden a little more than forty years."

"But Mrs. Gibson, I don't even know what he's doing."

"As a matter of fact, Christine, neither do I."

"I've always thought him capable of doing something really good."

"And you've been disappointed?"

"The trouble is, I don't know what he's done. I'm out of touch with him. I've given myself to Christ."

"How nice! And that's why you no longer attend the services in Pastor Pruitt's church?"

"Yes. Those people don't know what happiness is — the happiness I know now. So how can I be sure that my prayers are helpful?"

"Do you want me to tell Christopher that he is your prayer burden?"

"Oh no. Don't tell him I called you. Don't tell anyone."

"Of course you know that I won't tell anyone you called. But you shouldn't be modest. It may have been your prayers — rather than mine — that saved him for a second marriage."

"I didn't know he had married again."

"Yes. About a week ago in London. An English girl."

"I have to go pick up my children, and I'm late

now." Christine's voice was reproachful, as it might have been if Ada had talked too long. "They go to a Christian school."

Ada, wondering how the school where Marty had been a teacher and Christopher his favorite pupil could have been, by any name, better, now knew she could count it among her many blessings that the prayers of Christine West had not made her Christopher's wife.

On the following day, Venus shone alone in the clear morning sky. More than this, it was Friday — a day so remarkably different from all other days of the week that, in order to refresh her memory, Ada carried *Webster's New International* to her breakfast table in the kitchen and read aloud, "Friday, the sixth day of the week; the day following Thursday. It is the Moslem sabbath. In some churches, especially the Roman Catholic Church, Friday is a day of abstinence, except when it coincides with certain feast days, as Christmas. Friday was long known as hangman's day, because it was the customary day for hangings."

It did not surprise her to read that "Friday-faced," a term meaning "having a sad or melancholy look," had become obsolete. Webster dutifully made clear the distinction between Frigg, the wife of Odin and guardian of both marriage and domestic life, and Freya, the sister of Frey and goddess of love and beauty. Nevertheless, Webster wrote, his countrymen continued to confuse one with the other.

In other words, Ada concluded, it had become customary for Frigg to take the children to Disneyland or the beach on Friday, while Freya went to the Marriott with Odin, or his human alter ego. She returned Webster's big dictionary to the bookcase and hurried to the barn to feed her pets.

That chore done, visions of a long day's work danced in her head. Indeed, between a field that should have been mown earlier in the week and housework that never was done, Ada hardly knew where to begin. And when she found the door by which she had left the house locked, she was both incredulous and Friday-faced.

In a less desperate dilemma she might have gone to the home of the neighbor who, on Monday, had restored her mailbox. But, Friday being a market day, he surely had gone to the city to sell the fruits of his labor. Ada found herself obliged to count the ways that her house, with its doors locked, could be entered.

One by one she surveyed the windows and remembered how their screens were secured, from the inside, by steel hooks and eyes. Then, to a realization that her small house seemed an impregnable castle something more distressing was added: the sky, clear at dawn, was dark with clouds and letting down rain. Still dressed in what she euphuistically referred to as "morning clothes," she now was not only besieging and beset but wet.

"Please, God, help me get into my house."

Ada remembered suddenly that a cellar window — one left open for ventilation — had not been locked into its frame, nor was the screen secured by hooks and eyes. It would be a simple matter to lift the screen from its moorings. So it proved to be, and she stretched out before the opening and backed into the cellar, landing on both feet with less difficulty than might have been expected.

She knew now that her house was not impregnable. No visions of the day's work danced in her head, and she could not imagine why, after thirty years of leaving that one door open, she had touched the bolt that locked it. But she did not let these riddles concern her. Rain had dashed her hopes of mowing a field, and it was Friday. She would change her wet clothes for dry ones, and celebrate. More exactly, she would put on the rose plaid coat that Marty had bought on one of their rare shopping trips — with a black stocking cap of the kind he used to wear — and go to the gift shop in town.

When she arrived, the rain had stopped and the streets were bright with sunshine. Across the street from the parking lot where Ada had left her car a moment before, a trucker was bringing his truck to heel while a tall man stood in the middle of the street directing him. The tall man reminded her of Marty. Physically, he resembled Marty very little. Their height, however, was the same, and he was doing what Marty, in the same spot, might have done.

In profile, the man's expression was wistful, as though the trucker's skill had reminded him of a private sorrow too deep for words, and his expression became vocal when Ada, still thinking of his likeness to Marty, smiled. "He set it on a dime," he said, reaching the curb where she was.

"He did, didn't he?" Ada said. "I envy everybody who can park parallel to the curb."

"I used to drive an eighteen-wheeler, and he's better than I was."

"It was an extraordinary performance. Surely."

Now that she thought of it, the fact that they had reached the corner together was extraordinary, too.

"If you're new in town, there's a place here where we might have lunch," he said, looking wistfully to their right.

"I'm not new in town," Ada said. "And I haven't time for lunch."

After hesitating briefly at the corner, however, they turned to the right and set off at a brisk clip in the same direction.

"I'm looking for a woman."

The statement was so forthright and his tone so far from being soft or sly that Ada smiled again, thinking how much like Marty this man was.

Then somewhat more quietly he said, "My room doesn't suit me. The way it is. Are you married?"

Ada, thinking of her neglected house, said nothing. What could she say? The door of the gift shop had already closed between them.

Saturday morning was clear, with every blade of grass in a coat of hoarfrost. Venus, once again, shone alone in a cloudless sky. It was a perfect day for mowing, and Ada, smiling the stoical smile with which she had left the church on Sunday, was carrying hay for the horse and looking down at a clump of *Aster multiflorus* in late flower beside the path when all of a sudden her right foot moved forward and dropped her whole weight on the foot that, just as suddenly, had folded beneath it.

A brisk breeze penetrated her woollen shirt. The little aster nodded beside her. She was too amazed to move. An interval of time passed in which only the aster moved. Then, without moving her lips, Ada said, "O Father in Heaven, please don't let my ankle be broken."

Alone with an aching ankle, she must carry her own hide to market. Not only was she alone and in pain, she was out of sight. She must get to the house, where the telephone was. And that Ada did. Her ankle was painful, but surely not broken. It would not have helped her walk to the house if it had been broken. So, indeed, there was no need to call the doctor. After a short rest, she would mow the field.

In the afternoon the sky was clear, as it had been at dawn. Flowers of the field that all through the summer had bowed whenever the mower came close to them now waited stiffly to be cut down. The summer was gone and the winter coming. The chill breeze still penetrated her woollen shirt. She was an old woman, and invisibly tucked away in the Nesbits' van there was an undeveloped film to prove it.

But of course it had been a good week. And what might have happened without the prayers of Pastor Pruitt's congregation, Ada would never know.

A Gift of Time

WHENEVER ADA saw them crossing the lawn between the house and the woods, she counted the quail. Doing this was an expression of a concern for animals she had shared with her mother, who, although tolerant of her own kind, seemed to have loved those creatures God created earlier. And now, with her back close to a wall of the old house they had shared until her mother's death (on the last night of September in Ada's fifty-first year), Ada counted the quail again. All were full-grown and ran close to one another, without exchanging the small talk that might have alerted a cat to their presence. Ada had counted fifteen yesterday, and today the number was fourteen. It was the little one, with the light brown feathers, that Beauty — a pregnant calico — had brought, as a gift, to the back door for Ada.

The quail had reached a big rock, where Ada fed them, and the sound of cheerful conversation was in the crisp air; but the joy of counting the quail was gone. Gone, too, was the warmth from the wall behind her. The silver-lined leaves of her favorite swamp maple were red. Soon it would shed its leaves and these precious days in October with them. Unfortunately, a sense of time's passing had come to her late in life and was not yet appreciated by those widowed friends who called her to the telephone, in the middle of a busy day, and asked, in voices reminiscent of Gray's *Elegy*, "Are you all *right*?"

Not only was this question, in her opinion, impertinent, it was — even with the conversational gift she had inherited from her father — a very difficult one to answer. When, truthfully, she said, "*I don't know*," questions even more tedious followed. Only once in a blue moon had it occurred to the caller to say, "I understand. We have no way of knowing when we are *right*, do we?"

Ada's telephone, in fact, was ringing when she set a basket of lawn clippings on the porch, where, a lifetime ago, her mother had grown red geraniums and white alyssum in a wooden tub. The caller, as it turned out, was not a widowed acquaintance but Christopher, and he said, "Were you asleep, Mother? I was ready to hang up the phone."

"I was in the yard, watching the sun go down."

"You don't sound happy."

"I've been happier."

"Can I help?"

"Would you like to be the model for Painters Limited next week?"

"I've never been a model."

"Neither have I. And they really want *you*. The supply of available celebrities being short."

"Really? But I'm not available next week."

"Neither am I. October is too good to be given away. What can I do?"

"Is this gift of time important to you?"

"Only because Melita has suggested it and I have a sense of obligation on account of her giving me a picture of Max begging for an apple to eat."

"But you did buy a frame for Melita's painting and hung it above the fireplace. Wasn't that enough?"

"I thought so."

"I agree."

"Melita says I'll be paid for being a model. What shall I do?"

"Do you need money?"

"No. I have your last gift and my bills are all paid."

"Then what's wrong?"

"It's October. And the leaves are beginning to fall. Lost time is never found. We *know* that. I'm still expecting to find some of the time I've lost."

"Oh — why not take the time and be a model and see yourself as others see you?"

"I hate surprises."

Christopher, at this point, sighed audibly — as he always did when that twenty minutes he had set aside for a telephone visit was gone. "What have you been up to today, Mother?"

"I rode the lawn mower around the house, raked some of the grass for Max, and watched the sun go down. What did you do — today?"

"After all morning in the studio finishing the *New Yorker* cover I told you I wanted to do, I raked leaves and ran them through the shredder. For next year's mulch."

"That's good."

"Would you like to have a leaf shredder, Mother?"

"No. Thanks."

"I'll be looking forward to seeing you as Melita sees you."

"Goodbye, Christopher. See you soon?"

Ada returned the old-fashioned black telephone to its dusty cradle and went to the fireplace, where, above its mantel, Melita's painting of Max had replaced Christopher's seascape with sandpipers on a beach of yellow sand. Max, as Melita had seen him, was not the handsome hunter that had cantered into

Ada's heart during Marty's long illness; nor was he the gentle pet she fed three times a day. In his stylish gray coat, Max had the look of those riderless mounts that, unfed, wait on a battlefield for their fallen owners to take them home. Ada, having accepted Melita's view of Max and bought a modest frame for it, continued to find the painting a source of pain. The fact that the real Max, with cheerful prehension of her occasionally dilatory delivery of evening snacks, had left the corral bar and begun to graze in the meadow did, however, delay her delivery of the basket of lawn clippings until morning, and allowed Ada to go to bed. Waiting for sleep, she recalled her mother's habit of closing her eyes whenever Ada spoke to her of matters that she thought might be of mutual interest and that, unfortunately, were not.

Her mother's speech had tended to be cryptic and (in a *ménage* where the men were encouraged to speak freely of their own interests and, without encouragement, read both the Scripture and the newspaper aloud) memorable. For example, there had been a time when, after her mother had braided Ada's heavy hair and fastened the two wide plaits with big bone pins so that they were, in reality, a crown, she said, "It's bad luck to see yourself over the shoulder of another person, in a mirror."

Then, without a word of explanation, she had gone

to the kitchen and packed a lunch for Ada to take to school. At another time, when Ada was looking into the blue-tinted mirror that hung in the parlor, her mother had said, "I don't know why *they*" — Ada's paternal grandparents — "had so *many* mirrors." This statement, too, had bemused Ada. Had it been a question, Ada might have answered, "They had *four* mirrors because there were *four* of them: Pop, Grandma and Granddad, and Aunt Kate, the one you think I'm *like*. How could they have put on their hats and gone to church without four mirrors?"

Ada's father, although he repeatedly read from the Bible on the subject of "childish things" and the wisdom of discarding them, had not mentioned the mirrors. One of her most poignant memories was of her father, in the last month of his life, going from a bed he, throughout the fifty-six years of his marriage, had slept in with her mother to "see himself" in a small mirror that was above the washstand in their bedroom.

One by one, Ada had taken the mirrors to her attic. The last to go was the one that, during her father's illness, had hung in her parents' bedroom. Before retiring it to the attic, however, Ada had hung it in the little room, now a bathroom, where she was born. There Marty and Christopher could see themselves while shaving, and she, with a brief glance, had seen what she wanted to see — a face that, like her father's, would be fair and free of wrinkles for as long as she lived.

Christopher, while shaving, had said, "I like the new mirror. It pulls the bathroom together."

"Not to mention all the people who see themselves in it."

"Really, Mother?"

"Yes. All sorts of people."

"Who else sees themselves in this mirror?"

"I have visitors. One of your father's old friends stops by once a year and goes to the bathroom before he leaves. And, then, we have visits by your children and their friends."

"I hope that your grandchildren aren't too much trouble?"

"Of course they aren't troublesome. But I can't help thinking that they have better things to do than visiting this place."

"Doesn't this place belong to them? In a way?"

"Why do I find that so easy to forget?"

"I'm finished in the bathroom, Mother." And Christopher, his shaving done, had gone into the guest room and closed its door between them.

Several days later, when Ada brought breakfast to the cats that habitually waited on the back porch for their

meals, she saw that Beauty had given birth to five
black kittens. Since it was October and the night a
cool one, a young tom had joined the mother and her
kittens in a cardboard box that Ada had intended, as
soon as she had the time, to fold and tie with similar
boxes for recycling. It was not her intention, certainly,
to fill it with cats. So that when Melita, stopping by to
pick her up later in the morning, accused her of cruelty, she was offended.

Having driven her station wagon into Ada's yard
and left the engine running, Melita said, "Don't you
know it's cruel to have all those kittens?"

"Cruel" was one of the words with an implication
of "judgment" and therefore alien to the daughter of a
man who had read the Bible aloud. *"Judge not, that ye
be not judged. For with what judgment ye judge, ye shall be
judged."* Had time permitted, she might have added,
since her memory from childhood had been good,
*"Thou hypocrite, first cast out the beam out of thine own eye;
and then shalt thou see clearly to cast out the mote out of thy
brother's eye."* Cruelty, in other words, was a result of
judgments like the one that had allowed Melita to
leave her wagon's engine running, with the air condi-
tioner burning a patch of Ada's lawn, and the one that
had prompted Ada's mother, having found a nest full
of kittens in the haymow, to take an axe from the
woodpile to chop off their heads. For her beautiful

mother, the latter was one of the rites of spring and no more cruel than church attendance in a new white dress and patent leather pumps, on Easter Sunday, might have been for Ada.

"Cruel? The word that occurred to me was 'expensive.' Like forgetting to turn off your car's engine. If Beauty had consulted me, I would've told her how much a case of cat food costs."

"Beauty should have a hysterectomy."

"These are wild cats, Melita. Had Beauty's mother been *tamed,* she wouldn't have had Beauty."

"So?"

"I don't want a tame cat living in the house all of the time, or dying at my feet — like my poor Ezra — because he trusted people. Ezra was shot by a man who thought there were too many cats in the world. I've been feeding an army of wild cats ever since."

"Well, are you ready to leave your wild cats?"

"Now that they've had their breakfast, yes."

Once seated and safety-belted beside Melita in the station wagon, Ada considered the prospect of being a model for the members of Melita's art class. It was a warm and sunny day, like the March day when Ezra died, and, having promised this gift of time to Painters Ltd., she had nothing to do but look forward to a good morning. When Ada was thirty years old, her mother, holding the proofs of a recent visit to the photographer's studio of her choice, had said, "Ada, your *look* hasn't changed. It's the same as it always was."

Ada, assuming that her mother had in mind an agreeable "look," had not thought it necessary to question her at the time. When Ada was more than sixty years old and Marty (who was almost seventy and already inclined to be repetitious) said, "You're still a good-looking woman. You'll always be a good-looking woman," she had believed him. And unlikely though it was that everyone in Melita's art class would agree with Marty, everyone would surely be as kind as the camera had been nearly fifty years ago.

The middle-aged brunette who greeted her at the workshop's entrance was businesslike, and the crisp hold she immediately took of Ada's left elbow indicated an urgency that Ada, at the moment, did not feel. Bright sunshine flooded the workshop, but its air was not kind. The would-be painters were setting up their easels and jousting for what seemed to them the right place to be, while Ada, with her escort, crossed the sunny room and mounted a platform where an old-fashioned fan-backed wicker chair stood awaiting its drapery of blue cloth and Ada.

Seated, with her feet settled into the huge footprints

that were drawn on the floor in front of the chair, Ada opened the book she had expected to read while serving as a model. Her head — although it had been adjusted by her escort to show the painters an alert, forward-looking profile — tilted to one side, the way her father's head invariably did when he sat, with a book, in his favorite chair. As the time went by, sunshine warmed the workshop considerably. Ada's eyes, not unlike her mother's in the later years of her life, had an uncontrollable tendency to close. In a determined effort to stay awake, Ada tried to recall happier times and portraits that had required almost no effort on her part.

The first, a studio photograph taken when Ada was three months old, showed a sated and stoical baby in a short white dress.

The second, taken in the same studio when she was two years old, was more agreeable. Her coiffure was not all that the hired girl, who had curled Ada's straight hair for the photograph, could have hoped it would be. But the face between her ragbag curls was *fair*. More than that, her second photograph revealed a trait that an adult acquaintance who did not know Ada well might have thought to be a lack of patience. An intense gaze into the camera's eye and a rigidly extended right arm — with an overblown artificial rose in its clenched fist — seemed to say that Ada suspects the man who gave her the rose is an "Indian giver," and that, although he has gone into hiding under a black cloth, she would like to return that gift *now*.

But Ada's relationship with both man and camera improved and, instead of the rose, in her next photograph she is holding a small bouquet of lilies-of-the-valley her mother had gathered on the farm and brought to the city for Ada to hold. These flowers are hers and she holds them loosely because, in the interim, Ada has learned it is the only way to hold living things. At the same time, she stands with her left foot forward beside the photographer's one-armed chair and smiles the one-sided smile that had come — naturally — when the man behind the camera said, "Smile, Ada. *Smile.* I'm afraid of a cross woman and mad dogs."

This happy recollection of Ada's ended when a schoolroom bell rang and Melita announced to the room of painters, "We have coffee and goodies for you. Come and get it."

Then, out of a maze of abandoned easels, the no-nonsense woman who had settled Ada into the fan-backed chair returned to the dais and, for a second time, took a firmer hold on Ada's arm than seemed to be necessary. But she did not say, as younger women often did, "Watch your step, Mrs. Gibson. We don't want you to fall." After they descended from the dais together, she said, with a wave of her hand in the direction of the coffee table, "Now you'll have time to see what we've done."

"With some encouragement, I would've been a painter," Ada told her.

"What happened?"

"It's a long story."

"As the mother of Christopher Gibson, you must be very proud."

"Are you asking a question, or giving me an order?"

"Neither. The question, if I wanted to pry, might be: Is Christopher *happy*?"

"As his mother, I *must* believe that he is *happy*." Then, with the last crumb of a pineapple Danish in her mouth, Ada asked the way to the restroom. And when her feet had been returned to the chalk marks on the dais, her caretaker promised Ada that time would go more quickly now, and it did.

The school bell had rung a second time, signifying that her morning of modelling was over, and Ada, with her pay in hand, began to see what the painters saw. It was to be expected, she thought, that Melita — being of Hispanic descent — should have used the morning to represent Ada in the likeness of a local woman who, having been born in the province of

Pennsylvania and lived there a lifetime, tended to be suspicious of more recent occupants of the state.

"Don't take it too seriously," Melita said. "I always work with the right side of my brain and try to be kind."

"I know," Ada said, remembering their earlier conversation on the subject of Beauty and her kittens. "It is very difficult, I imagine, to be kind in *watercolor.*"

"It is," Melita agreed. "Now we'll see Mr. Trate's canvas. He works in oil with considerable success and has done more than three hundred self-portraits."

"You don't mean it."

At this point, an elegant blonde who very possibly had, like Mr. Trate, a gift for self-portraiture greeted Ada and said, "You are the mother of Christopher Gibson, aren't you, and his first teacher?"

Thinking that this woman, had she had a voice as well disciplined as her appearance, might have been Elsa in a production of *Lohengrin*, Ada said, "Yes. But Christopher's work habits were inherited from his father."

"We must go see Mr. Trate's portrait of you now," Melita whispered. Still whispering, she added, "*He* is our Rembrandt."

The next moment, standing at Melita's side and looking across Mr. Trate's left shoulder, Ada saw herself not as she had seen herself that morning in the new bathroom mirror, or in many friendly meetings with the camera, but as Mr. Trate, the Rembrandt of Painters Ltd., saw her on this lovely October day.

Mr. Trate did not smile when, aware of Ada's presence, he turned and said, "Mrs. Gibson, I'm going to take this portrait to my studio and do a little more work on it."

Did he think a willingness to "do a little more work" would undo the harm his "work" had already done? Ada's hair, like her father's, had lost its color prematurely, but when had she lost so much of it that her scalp was visible? Looking at Mr. Trate's canvas, she remembered a movie she hadn't thought of in years, and, with a dry smile, asked, "Have you ever seen *Lost Horizon*?"

"As a matter of fact, I saw a rerun on television recently."

"The one I'm seeing isn't on television."

Mr. Trate appeared to understand without taking offense. He said, "Leaving your own Shangri-la in the country must've been very difficult."

"It was."

"But you were one of our best models, and I hope you'll model for us again."

"That is nice to hear. It was Thoreau, I think, who said, 'To see what another person sees is a miracle.' I think I've survived my share of miracles."

"Then let me give you this. After I've done a little work on it."

"My house is small and its walls are filled with *things*."

"You're the mother of Christopher Gibson, aren't you?"

Able to smile at this familiar question, Ada said, "I am."

"He has a bigger house?"

"Yes, with a room where his wife hangs unfinished portraits."

"So I'll give your portrait to him — in exchange for one of his shore birds of New England."

The exchange took place in Mr. Trate's studio on a dark day in November. Ada's portrait, in an ornate frame of carved wood, had not been improved by the frame or the additional "work." Nor was it *kind*. It was an oil painting of a very old woman, with a liver-spotted face and a shocking pink scalp.

Solace

ADA DROPPED a lighted match into the heap of Christmas paper at the edge of her woods and watched its flame consume the red tissue in which one of several gifts from Christopher had been wrapped. It was a clear day, with a stiff breeze from the northwest. She wore faded blue jeans with unravelling cuffs and a red mackinaw that had belonged to Marty. An inch of snow had fallen during the night, and, against a cloudless sky, the balsam fir that Ada's mother had planted to add a touch of green to the gray woods gently waved its wide branches. With snow on the ground and the wind coming the way it was, the risk of setting fire to the woods was minimal, Ada thought. But even while she prodded the pile of paper with the staff she sometimes used to steady her steps when walking outdoors, a green pickup truck turned in her yard, and

Mr. Murdough, her nearest neighbor, jumped from the cab.

"I saw your fire," he said, "and thought it might be the woods."

"Oh, no, this is where I always burn my trash — very carefully," Ada said, and she turned to the youthful tricolored collie that earlier in the year she had bought from the custodian of the local animal shelter. "We love that woods, don't we, Peter Pup?"

"You know that woods has no fire lanes and there'd be no way for us to bring in a fire engine."

"I know that," Ada said. Mr. Murdough's unexpected arrival implied a need for his presence that Ada had not felt, and she did not smile.

"If you tell me where to find a bucket, I'll bring water from your spring to douse the fire when you leave."

Though Ada previously had been unaware of Mr. Murdough's resemblance to her late husband, she noticed it now. Their straight fine hair, their deep-set hazel eyes and jutting jaws were similar. Especially like Marty was Mr. Murdough's determination to help.

The April that followed Marty's death, Mr. Murdough had driven his tractor into a field where Ada was hand-raking newly turned ground prior to planting peas in it and, above the roar of the engine, shouted, "That's not the kind of work you should be doing. It's too hard for you." There had been no time for Ada to explain that on account of a recent thunderstorm the soil was too wet to be worked any way but by hand. Looking as determined as Marty might have under the same circumstances, Mr. Murdough had sent the tractor careering back and forth, while she stood by and saw her garden ruined. Then, without speaking, Mr. Murdough had driven away, and Ada, rake in hand, had retired from the field. From that moment to this winter day many years later, Ada had not returned to plant peas, though in summer she drove her own tractor-drawn mower into the field to cut a tangle of red clover and Queen Anne's lace that grew where peas might have grown.

In the face of Mr. Murdough's present determination, Ada managed a smile that felt dry, if not actually forced. "The spring is so close," she said. "I'll douse the fire, if necessary."

"Are you alone, Ada?"

"Yes, Mr. Murdough. I'm alone."

"I thought Christopher might have come. For Christmas."

"It's a long way for him to come, and I don't mind being alone on Christmas — or any day. In fact, I enjoy being alone. After all, we'll all be alone in our caskets."

"I've never thought of that, Ada, and I'm not sure that you should have."

"I often attend my funeral in imagination. It can make Christmas alone seem happy."

"I'll suggest it as an exercise for my mother the next time she complains of being left alone. My father, as you know, was no saint."

"And now she thinks he was? A saint?"

"Yes."

"I know how that is."

"But Marty *was* a saint."

"Not quite," Ada said.

"I never heard him say an unkind word about anybody."

"I did."

"He was a great man."

"He was a singular man, with the ability to lead his students and acquaintances to accept their own singularity. That is a rare gift."

"Mother worries about you — all alone."

"Tell her not to worry. The Wertz sisters have invited me to share their Christmas dinner. And tell her to be glad that her son lives so close."

"Be careful when you drive today. There's ice under the snow."

"You take care, and have a merry Christmas."

"A merry Christmas to you, too." Briskly, Mr.

Murdough returned to his truck and started in the direction of his mother's house with Peter Pup, barking, leading the way.

A family of yellow jackets had nested during the summer in the ground not far from where Ada stood with her back to the fire, and the sharp stinging pain in her right ankle recalled summer's several clashes with its members; indeed, Ada would have been no more surprised to see a yellow jacket taking leave of her than she had been by Mr. Murdough's arrival a few minutes earlier. Widowhood, it seemed to her, was more surprising than her marriage had ever been.

What Ada saw when she looked down was not an angry yellow jacket but a fringe of flame along the right cuff of her blue jeans.

To Marty, an unexpectedly painful happening had been either "a new experience," and therefore a kind of "blessed event," or, as the blooming rhodora had been for Emerson, "its own excuse for being." Though disinclined to share Marty's stoical acceptance of surprises, Ada managed to bow from the waist and, with calloused hands and a wry smile, stifle the flame. That done, she called the dog and went into the house with him. At this point, as she saw it, there was no need to douse the trash pile.

After her father's death, Ada had carried upstairs the cushioned maple chair she had given him for Christmas in 1934 and set it at the head of Christopher's bed. Abandoned, the bed and chair waited with an expectant air in the room where Christopher had slept. Actually, they had the look Ada saw, on her way down the hall, reflected in her bathroom mirror. It was the look of a person who, although obviously of less use than she formerly was, continued to expect well of the future. Holding the medicine cabinet door open, Ada was relieved to see that a magazine clipping Marty had pasted inside long ago was still there. She read it aloud while Peter Pup listened:

" 'Whether caused by flame or chemicals, a burn should be flooded with water immediately for approximately fifteen minutes. A burn caused by chemicals should be examined by a doctor as soon as possible.'

"The treatment will be simple as taking a bath," she said, and, having closed the medicine cabinet door, she opened both spigots of the bathtub. Much simpler, surely, than the application of apple butter and sliced raw potatoes, tied on with strips of an old sheet, which her mother had used when Ada had burned her arms in hot corn mush. How old had she been at the time? Three, perhaps? Ada remembered, as though it happened today, the corn's color — pure gold — in an iron kettle on the arrow-backed chair. She remembered, too, how, after an awkward struggle with the bandages, her mother, who seldom had time to hold her, had taken her in her lap and held her there until the pain was gone. Compared with that pain, the pricklings Ada felt while bathing her ankle were a discomfort, nothing more.

Ada was in the tub when the phone rang. "That's Lucy Wertz calling to say 'Are you still alive?' " Ada told Peter Pup. And when, nude and waterlogged, she climbed from the tub and crossed the hall to answer the phone, she found that the caller was indeed Lucy Wertz.

"Were you at the barn?" said Lucy.

"No, I was taking a bath."

"In that case, you should have your breathing fixed, Ada."

"After the pulmonary lab tests, Dr. Hutchinson told me not to worry about my slight emphysema."

"Then perhaps you need an evaluation of your heart."

"Have you forgotten the Holter monitor I wore for one whole day last year, and the digitalis Dr. Razzano prescribed?"

"You may need another prescription."

"Right now what I need is a towel."

"You are coming to have dinner with us, aren't you?"

"Yes, after I'm dressed. If I'm not there by twelve, start dinner without me. Mr. Murdough was here and said there are patches of ice under the blowing snow."

"We've seen a car go by the house this morning. The road is open."

Ada didn't argue with her. Never having learned to drive, the Wertz sisters had sold their husbands' automobiles and forgotten the difficulties of driving in wintertime completely, so that nothing Ada might have said on that subject would have been useful.

"We'll pray that you have a safe trip," Lucy said, adding, "Jane's hungry."

"I'll try to be there by twelve," Ada said.

At ten minutes before twelve, Lucy Wertz, seeing Ada's blue compact in the snow-covered driveway beside the house, opened the back door and, with a delight so shrill that a stranger unaccustomed to Lucy's way of greeting visitors might have fled to the safety of the woods, said, "Merry Christmas, Ada. It's good to see you."

Familiar though Ada was with Lucy's greetings, she had not learned to respond to them; so without a word she followed Lucy into the kitchen, where Jane was turning the yams in a glaze of butter and sugar.

There, in the voice that a moment before had wel-

comed Ada, Lucy said, "Go on into the living room
and wait until dinner is ready." To reinforce her com-
mand, Lucy led the way and, from the center of the
room, said, "Sit down and read until I call you."

"In which one of the chairs would you like me to
sit?" Ada asked, remembering Marty's saying to her,
"You can take the girl out of the country, but you
can't take the country out of the girl." Lucy, Balti-
more-born and for forty years a teacher in the public
schools of that city, was trying to take the country out
of the girl Ada no longer was.

Lucy said, "You may sit wherever you like."

But, of course, nothing could have been less true.
Given her own choice of a place to sit, Ada would
have stayed in the kitchen, where Jane was tending
the yams.

"Then I'll sit here," Ada said, moving toward a
very old Windsor chair that had the patina of age and
its frailty.

"That will be all right." The words came slowly, as
though Lucy, knowing Ada's weight, would have
preferred to have her sit on the davenport. But then,
speaking more crisply, she said, "Read this," and left
Ada on her own.

The magazine that Lucy handed to Ada was a
monthly publication intended to advertise the virtues
of that branch of Protestantism to which the Wertz

sisters belonged, and Ada dropped it, unopened, on the neat pile of magazines from which Lucy had taken it. That done, she sat down in the old Windsor chair and turned a critical eye on her surroundings.

The room was one she had known in childhood and remembered with great affection, because at that time a favorite aunt and uncle had owned the house and during her mother's illnesses had offered Ada the solace she needed. Later, when her mother had recovered, Ada went to visit Uncle Nathan and Aunt Elizabeth with her parents. On those festive occasions, she had been allowed to stay in the kitchen while meals were being prepared and, best of all, encouraged to feel that her being there was helpful.

"Will you bring the balloon-backed chairs from the parlor?" Aunt Elizabeth would say if her sons were at home from the city and extra chairs were needed for the table. Or in warm weather, when milk and butter had to be refrigerated in the spring ditch, she would say, "Run for the butter and cream, Ada. The dinner is almost ready."

It seemed to Ada as if all that was bright and warm in her memories of childhood had happened in this room. Now the room — with its newly plastered white walls and precious Persian rug — was bright without being warm. It was extraordinarily neat. But, remembering it as it had been seventy years ago, she resented this neatness. Both the piano and the book-case were gone, along with Uncle Nathan's Boston rocker, where Aunt Elizabeth sat to mend his socks by the light of a huge kerosene lamp. Gone, too, was the horsehair sofa — that wonder of slippery elegance — where Ada herself sat while her cousin Isaac played the piano. The room had held a round stove, with nickel-plated extensions to warm cold feet. And Ada had not wanted to be in the kitchen.

Her wait, happily, was not long, and when she joined Lucy and Jane in the dining room her plate had been filled.

"We prefer chicken to turkey," Jane said. "We hope you do, too."

"I like both. This looks lovely," Ada said.

"Harvey liked ham," Lucy said. " What did Marty like?"

"Hamburger with cream sauce," Ada said.

"Bless his heart."

Seeing that the sisters had closed their eyes and bowed their heads in the silent blessing ordinarily asked by them, Ada inaudibly said, "Dear Lord, bless this house and help me to get home."

When their plates were as clean as good appetites could make them, Jane passed the fruitcake and Christmas cookies, while Lucy brought hot water to make instant coffee in their expectant cups. Meanwhile,

Ada wondered who now alive in this world could bake mince pie the way her mother had.

When the table had been cleared and Ada spoke of leaving, Lucy said, "Why, child, you've hardly said a word. You must tell us how Peter Pup is."

"Peter Pup is fine."

"And you?"

"I'm lucky to be here."

"Aren't we all?" Lucy said. " It's so beautiful here."

Jane, with a faraway look in her eyes, agreed, and said, "Yes, it is beautiful here. I was born in the middle class and expect to stay in it."

Ada laughed at this. "Middle class" was a term she seldom used, and if anyone had asked her where in America's complicated society she belonged, she would have said, "I don't know." Once, years ago, at a picnic on the church lawn, after telling Ada that both of her parents had migrated from Berlin to Baltimore, Lucy had asked, with an anxious look, "You are German, aren't you?"

Ada had said, "My father always told me you can't measure a snake while it's running." Remembering her rudeness on that occasion and hoping to make amends now, Ada said to Lucy, "I caught fire this morning."

"How, child?" Lucy and Jane said together.

"I was burning trash where I always do, and watching Peter Pup herding Mr. Murdough into his truck, when the fire took hold of my jeans."

"What did you do? Did you roll on the ground? Did you call Mr. Murdough?" They spoke as one excited person.

"I smothered the flame with my hands."

"How could you?"

"Easily. It was a small flame, and I was lucky."

"Yes, you were lucky."

"And now I really must be going. I'm expecting Christopher to call."

"We'll call you tonight to see how you are."

Ada wanted to tell Lucy that another interrogation on the subject of her health would be an invasion of privacy but found herself saying, "Thanks for the lovely dinner. It made a perfect day."

"Come back soon," Lucy said. "Be sure to drive carefully."

On the ice of the Wertz sisters' driveway the wheels of Ada's car spun for some time before she reached the sun-dried road. She was still ten miles from home and knew that snow had drifted into the road along the way. There was one small plain where, having had previous experiences with snowdrifts, Ada expected her car to stall, but when she got there, instead of a snowdrift she found two neat piles of snow, with the road, clear as could be, between them.

Seeing the green truck up the road, she knew the man leaning on his shovel in the truck's shadow was Mr. Murdough. He was smiling in the complacent way that Marty smiled when, another day of teaching behind him, he would walk from his parked car across the lawn toward their back porch.

Ada stopped her car. "What do I owe you, Mr. Murdough, for opening the road?" she asked.

"That's what neighbors are for."

"In that case, thank you very much. I want to be home by the time Christopher calls."

"You'll have no trouble from here on."

"You're a saint."

"Any time you need help — day or night — call me," Mr. Murdough said as Ada's car gathered speed.

Words like "that's what neighbors are for" were part of the local language and not to be taken without a grain of salt. They were, however, a comfort to hear. At home, Peter Pup would be waiting, and that, too, was a solacing thought.

When Christopher called, Ada was resting in the kitchen with the dog. When she told Christopher that on that very day both Mr. Murdough and a fire had visited her, he asked, "Was the fire Mr. Murdough's fault? Did he push you toward the trash pile?" Christopher's voice suggested a blend of genuine concern and amusement.

This was a form of banter she had used when Christopher was a child and he, out of a sense of loyalty — or was it anxiety? — still used.

"Have you seen a doctor?" Christopher wanted to know.

"On Christmas?"

"How *is* your health, Mother?"

"You know my heart is damaged?"

"I know. Dr. Hutchinson told me."

"And there is lung damage, too, and a considerable loss of memory."

"The way you describe it, it almost sounds jolly."

"But none of my doctors look amused when they see me. Have I lived too long?"

"Certainly not," Christopher said with conviction.

"That's nice to know."

"We'll talk again on New Year's Day, Mother. In the meantime, don't stand too close to the fire."

"Thanks for being a good boy, Christopher," Ada said, and settled the receiver back in its cradle.

Peter Pup, relieved of the obligation to eavesdrop, went to his nest and, with a deep sigh, curled up to sleep. Ada, after going to the window and making certain that it was the evening sun and not a brush fire burning among the gray trees beyond the old fir, turned on her radio and sat down to hear the last of the Christmas music. A shadow of the barn lay on the field, where the fringes of dry buck grass moved like the gentle flame that had felt like the sting of a yellow jacket and, like the pain of a yellow jacket's sting, was soon gone.

The Question

"Will you put me to sleep — when I become too troublesome?"

"No," Dr. Mordecai said. "I don't do that."

"You could be one of the licensed criminals that my father said all doctors are."

"Some are. Not all."

"If I can choose a predator to end my life, I'd prefer it to be you."

"I'm going to help you do the things you want to do. What has become of the other doctors you've known?"

"I've survived them."

This, like the question with which Ada's visit to Dr. Mordecai had begun, was intended to be amusing. It was true, however, that she had survived many of the doctors of her acquaintance and now expected Dr. Mordecai to outlive her.

"Has anyone ever told you that you are a remarkable person?"

"No. Not that I can remember."

In the silence that followed, while Dr. Mordecai compared the nurse's current recording of Ada's weight and blood pressure with her earlier recordings, Ada recalled a time when her mother, in one of their mother-daughter talks, said, "You are *odd*." And she, knowing how much her mother enjoyed wearing a hobble skirt in a neighborhood where she alone was the owner of one, had thought it nice to be odd.

Later, the two roommates she had had at Red Rock College told her — as if, having asked for their advice, they were giving her the benefit of a sudden perceptivity — "You are wound too tight, Ada," and "Don't marry Marty. You can do better." A classmate, seeing her with Marty in their senior year, had shared her opinion with others; it was "There is the most *indifferent* girl I've ever known."

Amusing as these judgments were, it was enough to remember them now with a smile. None of them had implied that she was, in any way, "a remarkable person." Nor did a question she overheard Marty's Aunt Gertrude ask him — during a visit early in his marriage — imply that Ada was "odd," "wound too tight," or "indifferent." The question was "Is Ada as *lazy* as she used to be?" Hearing it then, Ada had not been amused. And she was not smiling — sixty years later — when an older woman, who was retired from a lifetime of teaching in the public schools, declared, while "reaching out and touching" Ada by telephone, "You could have been a teacher. If your father hadn't *spoiled* you." This is not to say that Ada did not regret her failure to have been a teacher; without her father's understanding of that failure she, almost certainly, would have tried to follow Marty into the profession that, in her father's thirteen years' practice of it, required, he said, "the strength of Samson, the wisdom of Solomon, and the patience of Job." Knowing her lack of those gifts, he had told her, "You are not *well* enough to be a teacher." And with that, Ada agreed.

Dr. Mordecai, having closed the folder on his desk, looked across the narrow space between them. "Don't forget that last year, at this time, you were dying."

"I thought I was resting, with an injured back, on my bed at home."

"And now look at you."

The look Dr. Mordecai shared with her then was not "a black marble stare" of the sort Picasso had made famous; nor was it the absent-minded gaze that she, in the years without Marty, both expected and welcomed in her meetings with unrelated men. Dr. Mordecai's look *related*. He was a doctor of whom at least one middle-aged woman, with grandchildren in his care, had said, "He's an adorable man."

Ada had come to him for "a second opinion" when a drug prescribed by the doctor who had undertaken to reduce her blood pressure readings not only had failed to reduce her blood pressure but had increased a painful sensitivity to sunshine. The years since that first meeting with Dr. Mordecai had aged them both — naturally. Yet whenever he lifted her right foot to his knee and turned down the top of Ada's knee-high hiking hose to measure the amount of water that her weakening heart had allowed to collect there on the day of her brief visit, Ada remembered Cinderella and said, "My right leg tends to swell ever since I fell out of a cherry tree when I was eight years old. I don't think a glass slipper will fit its foot."

"I don't have a glass slipper."

"That's just as well. I hope I haven't wasted your time. I don't want to waste your time — *or* my money. You know that, don't you?"

"Yes," he said while, with her feet planted side by side on the green carpet, she pried herself free of the chair and stood beside that desk where, the moment before, Dr. Mordecai had been writing in her chart.

Waiting there for her sense of balance to return, Ada asked, "Why do I walk the way I do?"

Dr. Mordecai's voice, coming from the shadowy room where his food supplements were stored, was crisp and a little louder than she had expected it to be: "You walk the way you do because you are eighty-four years old."

And since it was unlikely that he knew how strange walking, at her age, could be or, knowing the awful truth, could suggest a remedy, she decided to move, with the fingertips of her right hand skipping ahead on the chair rail, in the direction of the desk where her account must be settled. That done, she would leave this building and settle into the sprightly little Buick Christopher had given her, when she was only eighty years old, and go home. Her appointments with Dr. Mordecai were more costly and time-consuming than they had been seven years ago. Was this a way of preparing her for death? Were these office visits, as Melville, speaking of death, said: "A launching into the region of the strange Untried; a first salutation to the possibilities of the immense Remote, the Wild, the Watery, the Unshored"? Or was this good-looking youngster truly able, as he had said, to help her do the things she wanted to do? This was the question Ada wanted to ask and he, unasked, had not answered.